Christmas 2020

Dear Friends,

In the spring of 2020 Wayne and I took an educational cruise up the Columbia River. This was not the luxury cruise I had expected. It was more like adult summer camp. No swim deck, no phones, no TV, no Internet, but lots of fun. Two great book ideas came from this experience. One of which you are holding in your hands.

Wayne and I have traveled up the Amazon, and several of the experiences mentioned here are ones we participated in ourselves. We've also been to Antarctica. Wayne likes to take me to exotic locations that don't take credit cards. We're at the point in our lives when we want adventure before dementia.

This book is dedicated to Nancy Jacuzzi (yes, *that* Jacuzzi!). We met on a tour bus on our cruise in South America, became instant friends, and have traveled together on two other tours. It was with Nancy that I went kayaking in Antarctica. And yes, there were whales. And penguins. And seals. She is a dear and treasured friend.

I hope you enjoy the story of Everly and Asher. And may your holidays be merry and bright.

As always, one of my greatest joys as an author is hearing from my readers. You can reach me through all the social media platforms, or by snail mail at P.O. Box 1458, Port Orchard, WA 98366.

Holiday blessings,

Debbie Macomber

Debbie MACOMBER

Jingle all the Way

sphere

SPHERE

First published in the United States in 2020 by Ballantine Books, an imprint
of Random House, a division of Penguin Random House LLC, New York
First published in Great Britain in 2020 by Sphere

1 3 5 7 9 10 8 6 4 2

A CIP catalogue record for this book is available from the British Library.

ISBN 978-0-7515-8114-0

Printed and bound in Great Britain by Clays Ltd, Elcograf S.p.A.

Papers used by Sphere are from well-managed forests
and other responsible sources.

Sphere
An imprint of
Little, Brown Book Group
Carmelite House
50 Victoria Embankment
London EC4Y 0DZ

An Hachette UK Company
www.hachette.co.uk

www.littlebrown.co.uk

To Nancy Jacuzzi,
a woman of extraordinary shopping skills,
a connoisseur of fine wines,
a culinary expert,
a jigsaw puzzle master,
and
a treasured friend

Jingle all
the Way

CHAPTER ONE

Everly Lancaster was ready to explode. Her assistant, Annette, the very one Jack Campbell, her business partner and CEO, had highly recommended she hire, who also happened to be his niece, had made yet another crucial mistake. One in a long list of costly errors. This time, however, this Gen Z, spoiled, irresponsible, entitled young woman had gone too far.

Annette Howington had mortified Everly in front of five hundred real estate brokers.

"It's really not that big a deal," Annette insisted, smiling as if to suggest this had all been a small misunderstanding. "You did fine without your speech."

The awards banquet held in the posh Ritz-Carlton Hotel, half a block off Chicago's Magnificent Mile, honored the top brokers for the online real estate company Easy Home. As Everly stepped onto the podium to deliver her carefully crafted speech, she discovered that her empty-headed assistant had downloaded the wrong talk and graphics. As a result, Everly had been forced to stumble through what she remembered of it. To her acute embarrassment, she'd sounded ill prepared, fumbling over words and names.

Everly was always at the top of her game. She did not stand up before a crowded banquet room and make a fool of herself.

"Not that big a deal?" Everly repeated, after the banquet. Annette had tried to escape without Everly noticing. No such luck. Everly had the assistant in her sights, and no way was she letting Annette sneak out.

"This is the last straw," Everly said, managing to keep her anger under control. "I've given you every opportunity. I'm afraid I'm going to have to let you go."

"You're firing me?" Annette asked in utter disbelief. "But I'm doing the best I can." For emphasis, she added a loud sniffle. "You've never liked me. From the day I started you've been demanding and critical." Her eyes filled with tears as if that would be enough to convince Everly to change her mind. She sniffled again for extra measure, her shoulders making dramatic shudders.

No way was Everly going to allow Annette to turn this on her. "Your best isn't good enough. You don't possess the skills I need in an assistant. The first thing Monday morning

I'll explain to your uncle that you will no longer be working with me or Easy Home." Everly couldn't think of a single position this ditzy girl could handle in the entire company. She'd even managed to mess up answering the phone on more than one occasion.

Annette's tears evaporated and a cocky expression came over her. "Uncle Jack won't let you fire me. I'm his favorite niece."

Everly gritted her teeth. "We'll see about that."

With a confident flair, Annette whirled around and stormed straight to her mother, who stood in the rear of the ballroom, waiting for her daughter. Everly watched as Annette burst into tears and pointed at Everly. A horrified look came over Louise Campbell as she started to weave her way around the tables toward Everly.

Bring it on, sister, Everly thought, more than prepared to face this tiger mom. Before that happened, however, Everly was waylaid by one of the brokers with a question. When they finished speaking, both Annette and her mother were nowhere to be seen.

Everly had a reputation to protect. She'd worked hard to make Easy Home the success that it was. What Annette said about Jack defending her was a worry, but nothing she couldn't handle.

The problem was Jack and his easygoing, everything-will-take-care-of-itself attitude. They'd met in college while getting their business degrees. Jack was the creative mastermind.

Everly possessed the business savvy and drive to take his idea of an online real estate company for Chicago and put it in motion. Six years ago they'd formed a partnership, and, working side by side, the concept had grown at a furious rate. With Everly at the helm, overseeing the everyday operations, Jack was content to rest on his laurels after handling the media-facing and investors. Basically, he left the running of the company to Everly. And she'd let him.

First thing Monday morning, Everly approached Jack in his office. "We need to talk about Annette."

Jack barely glanced up from his in-office putting green, where he stood, gauging the distance between the golf ball and the hole.

When he didn't respond, Everly said, "I've given her every opportunity, Jack. I'm letting her go."

Jack, ever willing to overlook his niece's complete lack of professionalism, sighed loudly. "I know. I know. And I appreciate the way you've taken her under your wing. This is my sister's girl and it means the world to Annette to have the chance to learn from you. You realize she idolizes you."

Then God help her if the young woman intentionally had it out for her, Everly mused. "Jack, take your eye off that golf ball and look at me. Favorite niece or not, I'm done."

Jack looked up and his eyes widened. "Annette was named after my mother."

"I don't care if she was named after the Statue of Liberty, I refuse to work with her a minute longer. The girl is incompetent."

His shoulders sagged. "Please reconsider."

That he would ask infuriated Everly. "No."

"No?" Jack looked both crestfallen and shocked.

After mentally reciting the alphabet, she tried again. "I know you love Annette and want to please your sister, but I'm the one left to deal with this pampered, entitled, inept girl."

Jack pretended not to hear and did a couple of practice golf swings. "I'll think on it," he said, as if this was his decision.

Which was so Jack. He had tunnel vision and refused to deal with unpleasantness, especially anything having to do with his family.

"Great. You want to keep Annette working here, then I have an idea," Everly said with an exaggeratedly cheerful note. "Make Annette your assistant."

"I can't do that," Jack insisted, leaning against his putter. "Maryann has worked with me from the beginning. Besides, Annette is family." To his credit, Jack looked uncomfortable. When he glanced up, a pleading expression came over him. Everly knew that look. He was trying to figure out a way to change Everly's mind. That wouldn't work. Not this time.

Jack smiled. "I know you're upset, and you have a right to be. It was a silly mistake, but Annette apologized . . ."

silly mistake? She apologized?" If he defended this nit-
one more time, Everly was going to walk out the door
d leave the running of the company to him and see what
e had to say then.

"You're not listening to me, Jack. I. Have. Reached. My.
Limit."

Jack stared at her for a long moment. "I'm pleading with
you, Everly. Give her one more chance, that's all I'm asking.
With a fresh start I believe Annette will prove her worth.
Don't make a hasty decision."

Hasty decision? Had Jack lost his ever-loving mind?

He must have noticed the stubborn expression she wore,
because he added, "Remember, this is her first job out of college. We all make mistakes. You did. I did. We were fortunate
that people believed in us. Is it so much to ask that we give
my sister's daughter the same opportunity?"

"Admit it, Jack, anyone else would have been out the door
weeks ago."

"Come on, Everly," Jack pleaded again.

Everly shook her head. "What you fail to realize is that
Annette not only let me down, but she's failed you, and this
entire organization. You aren't going to be able to turn this
around. I'm not changing my mind."

Having had her say, Everly left his office.

———

Annette sat at her desk, wearing the same cocky look she had at the banquet. The twerp knew her uncle would never fire her, and she thought this made Everly powerless. Everly hadn't built this company and earned the respect of this industry to let some kid win this war.

Jack followed Everly into her office. He paused long enough to close the door before facing her. After a moment, he leaned forward and braced both hands on the edge of her desk. "When was the last time you had a vacation?"

Of all the responses she'd expected from him, this one was a surprise. "A vacation?" she repeated. "What does that have to do with anything?"

"You're stressed out, and it's showing."

"Ya think?" she said with a huff. "I can't and won't tolerate incompetence. If anything, Annette is responsible for upping my stress level." She already had her hand on the phone to connect with HR. Whether Jack liked it or not, Annette was getting fired.

"Letting go of Annette will devastate my sister."

"Your sister?" she repeated, shaking her head. Jack's sister was the least of her worries.

"And Annette, too, of course."

"Apparently you didn't hear me. I gave Annette every opportunity. She doesn't have the skills or the maturity for this position."

;ive her one more chance," he urged, placing his hands
:aying position.

Everly adamantly shook her head. "I already have. I've
;id all I will on the subject."

"It's nearly December."

What did that have to do with any of this? "It doesn't
matter, Jack. My mind is made up."

Jack straightened and pointed a finger at her. "I want you
to take the entire month of December off."

"What? I can't . . ." It sounded like Jack had lost his
mind. No way could he deal with everything if she wasn't
around. The entire staff knew she was the problem-solver,
not Jack. Then again, maybe this was exactly the lesson he
needed.

The idea of sending her away for a month seemed to be
growing in his mind as he started to smile, looking pleased
with himself. "You need a break and I'm going to see that
you get one and that's final."

Everly frowned, wondering what had come over him.

"No buts, Everly. You're too valuable to me and this company, but your drive is smothering your compassion. We'll
somehow muddle through without you. Now book a vacation."

Her mouth opened and closed several times before she
swallowed. The entire month of December? It was Novem-
ber 30; she had no idea where she'd go or what she'd do.

Within a matter of days, she'd be bored out of her mind. This position consumed her every waking minute. Then again, there was always email. The team could reach her if necessary. Maybe it wasn't such a bad idea after all to let Jack take over the helm while she silently kept watch in the background.

Before she could stop him, although she wasn't sure she wanted to, he stepped out of the office and went directly over to Annette's desk. "I want you to book a vacation for Everly," he instructed. "Get her a cruise, somewhere tropical, with warm beaches where she can unwind."

Annette snapped to attention. "Right away," she said, eager to please her uncle. She immediately turned to her computer, and her fingers started typing away.

Everly put in a full day at the office. She rarely left before seven, long after everyone else had headed home. By the time she reached her Chicago condo, it was close to eight. For dinner, she generally picked up take-out on her way home. Her condo had an amazing view of Lake Michigan, although she seldom took time to gaze out the floor-to-ceiling windows. Seeing how little time she spent in her condo, it was more utilitarian than a real home. She had a few framed photos of her family here and there, but other than those, the space could have been a rental. And in fact, at one time it had been, until she was able to pick it up at a bargain price, thanks to Easy Home.

ce she ate her sushi with a glass of white wine, she
d on her white leather sectional and rested her bare feet
he matching ottoman, crossing her ankles. It'd been one
l of a day. She wasn't entirely sure she should take Jack up
n his offer. He seemed to feel she needed time away and he
wasn't far from wrong. She'd gone six years without a vacation worth mentioning. Oh, there'd been the occasional
weekend here and there with her college roommate Lizzy,
but those were rare now that Lizzy was married and had a
toddler.

Her phone rang and caller ID told her it was her mother.
For an instant, Everly was tempted to let it go to voicemail.
Then she decided if she didn't answer now, her mother would
simply try again later until Everly was forced to answer or be
destined to listen to a litany of voicemail messages.

"Hey, Mom," she said.

"Daisy." Just the way her mother said her given name,
which Everly hated, told her her mother wasn't pleased.

"Everything okay?" she asked, ignoring her mother's
tone.

"You were missed at Thanksgiving."

Her mother tossed guilt with the expertise of a no-hit
pitcher. "I'm sorry, I really am. I thought I could get away,
and then at the last minute something came up. I was forced
to stay in Chicago and deal with it." She crossed her fingers,
hoping her mother wouldn't inquire about that vague some-

thing. "I did let you know I couldn't make it." Coward that she was, she'd sent a text message.

"Was it the same something that prevented you from coming home for Christmas last year?" her mother asked pointedly.

This was the problem. Everly was the middle child in a family of five siblings. Two older sisters named Rose and Lily and two younger brothers, identical twins named Jeff and John. Everly had felt squished in between her sisters and brothers. Rose had Lily and Jeff had John and she was trapped in the middle. Everly needed elbow room, a way to prove she was her own person. She'd set out to do exactly that from the time she was two years old and learned to say the word no.

Lily used to tease her and claim Everly had been adopted. She might have believed it except the family resemblance was too strong. She had the same dark brown hair and brown eyes as the rest of her siblings. The same small curve in both her little fingers as all four of her siblings.

Her father blew it off by saying Everly was a typical middle child. Perhaps she was. From her earliest memories she'd been driven to be the best. If her job was to weed a garden row, she did it faster and better than any of her siblings did. She got top grades, was voted the most likely to succeed in her high school class, and was granted a full-ride scholarship to the University of Indiana, graduating magna cum laude.

Following graduation, she threw the entire force of her will and determination into getting Easy Home off the ground with Jack Campbell.

In contrast, her two sisters had both married young and started their families, and her brothers had joined their father in the farming enterprise. They had little in common with their upcoming-business-executive sister. When she was home it was as if they didn't have anything to talk about. Rose wasn't interested in how exciting the low home mortgage rates were and Everly had a hard time being excited little Rosie was cutting her first tooth.

"Are you going to answer the question?" her mother asked.

"Sorry, Mom, my mind was elsewhere."

"Will you or will you not be home for Christmas?" her mother asked, getting right to the point.

"Ah . . . home." If her family learned that she had the entire month of December off and she skipped the holidays for a second year running, there would be consequences. "I'll be home for sure."

"You promise?"

"Cross my heart. As it is, I'm taking a few days off."

Her words seemed to shock her mother. "You're taking a vacation?"

"That's what I just said."

"You don't sound happy about it."

That much was true. "Jack insisted I needed time away because I'm stressed out and he isn't far from wrong."

"Where do you plan to go?"

"Somewhere tropical, I guess . . . perhaps a cruise." She had never been one to idle away on a beach. The thought of all that wasted time depressed her. She didn't suntan easily and she detested the idea of sweating in a swimsuit.

"You make it sound like you're heading off to Guantánamo."

Everly smiled. "I'm not showing the proper amount of enthusiasm, am I?"

"You're not."

"The thing is, I'm not convinced I should go. Jack isn't as good at the business end of things as I am. I'm worried he'll mess up one or several of the major deals we have in the works."

"Then let him. You've carried your load and his for far too long."

The truth shouldn't feel this sharp. Her mother was right and Everly knew it. She'd gone back and forth on this vacation idea ever since Jack first mentioned it.

"It's up to you to make the most of this opportunity, Daisy," her mother continued. "You can make yourself miserable worrying about Jack and the business, or you can have the time of your life. It's up to you."

They ended the conversation with Everly promising to

spend Christmas on the farm and a determination to take her mother's words to heart.

As soon as Everly made an appearance Tuesday morning, Annette hurried to greet her, smiling as if she held a winning lottery ticket in her hand.

"I'm so grateful you've given me this chance to prove myself," Annette said. "Uncle Jack said it was more than I deserve, and I want to thank you." Her eyes sparkled with delight and were as round as the moon.

Everly eyed her warily.

"I found the perfect cruise for you." Annette clapped her hands so excitedly, it surprised Everly she didn't hop up and down. "There was a cancellation at the last minute and I grabbed it. You're going to have such a great time."

"And where is this cruise?"

"Brazil," Annette shouted and thrust her arms in the air as if she were a referee declaring a touchdown.

"Brazil," Everly repeated. Not bad.

Her smile deflated a little. "There's only one small problem. It leaves on Saturday."

Everly automatically shook her head. "That's impossible. I'd need shots and to get everything organized here at the office, plus pack." Her head was spinning like a bowling ball heading toward the gutter. No way could she make all that happen.

"That's just it!" Annette declared excitedly. "I've taken care of everything. I've got you an appointment this afternoon for your shots and had the prescription for the malaria pills filled, and"—she stopped to take in a deep breath—"I contacted the Brazilian consulate and they have agreed to expedite your visa application."

Annette clasped her hands and waited as if she expected Everly to applaud.

"Isn't she wonderful," Jack said, coming out of his office. He showed far more enthusiasm than Everly felt was necessary. "This is exactly what the doctor ordered." He smiled at Annette. "Good job."

"Thank you, Uncle Jack. It's refreshing to have someone believe in me." She stared pointedly at Everly.

It demanded effort for Everly not to roll her eyes.

"I'll go first thing on Friday morning to collect the travel documents," Annette said, "so you won't have a single thing to worry about."

The necessary shots were only part of what was needed. "What about my flight?"

"Booked," Annette announced, and shared a high five with her uncle. "I have you in business class, leaving O'Hare early Friday evening. Timing, unfortunately, is a tiny bit tight, but you should be able to make the ship when it sails Saturday afternoon."

Everly felt like everything was moving far too fast for her to keep up. "This is very last-minute . . . I'm not sure I can get everything together in such a short amount of time." She needed to get to her desk and handle the most pressing issues herself and delegate the rest. Jack might be her partner, but she didn't trust him to deal with the more stressing aspects of the business. She'd have to monitor him through emails to the members of her staff.

"One last thing," Annette said. "I've got all the paperwork filled out. All I need now is your passport."

"Excellent," Jack said with a wide grin.

For the next three days Everly nearly camped out at her office. She left several of the less delicate matters for Jack to manage. Easygoing Jack had shown far more interest in his golf game than in what was happening with the business. She handled nearly every aspect of the online business, although they were supposed to be partners. The rest of what was on her desk she delegated to her most trusted associates, spending hours explaining what needed to be done and what to expect.

On Friday morning, she woke to a snowstorm. The newscaster predicted ten inches before noon. If her flight was held up because of weather conditions, she would miss the cruise ship.

"What happens if my flight is delayed?" she asked Annette, once she got to the office. "Are there any other options?"

"No," Annette said, as if that had never entered her mind. "I was online searching for quite a while before I was able to find a flight that would get you to the dock on time."

"You did a fine, fine job," Jack complimented his niece, hugging her as if she'd scored an Olympic gold medal in gymnastics rather than managing to book Everly's travel arrangements.

"But the weather," Everly pointed out.

"No worries," Annette said, and handed Everly her travel documents. "I've been assured that the cruise will postpone the embarkation up to three hours if by some chance your flight is delayed. There shouldn't be a problem."

Three hours. She had a three-hour window to make the ship before it set sail.

"Excellent, Annette. You've thought of everything," Jack said, praising his niece yet again. "Brazil is perfect for Everly. Time to laze on a beach, bask in the sun, and let all the stress and worries of the job roll off her shoulders."

Like that was going to happen.

"What are you doing standing here?" Jack asked. "It seems to me you need to get packing. Be sure to stop off at the pharmacy and get sunscreen." He patted Everly on the back and escorted her to the elevator.

With more to do than her mind could comprehend, Everly headed home to pack. Two weeks on a cruise. Her flight was scheduled to fly out at five that afternoon, heading to Manaus, Brazil. According to the documentation, she had two stops and was scheduled to land at noon the following day. The cruise ship was scheduled to depart at three, plus she had that three-hour window if anything went awry.

Back at her condo, Everly pulled out her suitcase and tore through her closet. She needed summer clothes. The problem was her closet was full of business attire. She didn't own a single pair of shorts.

Everly detested all this rushing, afraid she would miss packing something vital. This wasn't the way she operated. She liked to plan everything out well in advance so she could be in control, but that option had been taken away from her. With only a few hours left to get ready, she packed what she thought would suffice, determined that she would shop for anything she needed once she arrived in Brazil.

By the time she left her condo the gently falling snow had turned into blizzard conditions. When she arrived at O'Hare, she discovered her flight had been delayed an hour. Fine, if the flight was canceled, then she had the perfect excuse to remain in town. Jack couldn't fault her for the weather. Already she was having second thoughts about leaving him in charge.

With nothing to do while she waited for her flight, she sat at the bar sipping wine, waiting for the latest update from the airlines. Two and a half hours after her scheduled departure time, her flight was called.

CHAPTER TWO

After two glasses of wine on an empty stomach, Everly was eager to close her eyes and do her best to relax. As much as possible she put the tight schedule out of her mind. If she missed the cruise, she missed the cruise.

At check-in she got the information for the two plane changes. One in Atlanta and another in São Paulo. She'd been assured by the airlines that there wouldn't be a problem with her connections, as she had a three-hour layover in Atlanta. Everly didn't want to dwell on how close she was cutting it to reach the ship on time. Already her mind was coming up with a contingency plan. If she missed the cruise, she would simply rent a hotel room and spend the next two weeks shopping, keeping in touch with everyone via email. She'd downloaded three business-type books she intended to read, so there would be plenty to occupy her mind. And for a guilty pleasure, she downloaded several romances as well.

As it turned out, she missed the connecting flight in Atlanta, but there was another flight leaving in two hours. That had an effect on the flight out of São Paulo as well. Thankfully, the airlines were able to find her a connection with a different airline that had her landing two hours into her three-hour window. The possibility of her missing this cruise was beginning to seem real. It would be tight, which would make the long overnight flight to Brazil too stressful to sleep.

Once she was on the plane in Atlanta, the woman sitting next to her in business class glanced over and smiled. The two struck up a conversation and Everly enjoyed chatting with another business executive. They had a lot in common. The flight attendant delivered them each a glass of champagne and a dinner menu before the flight's departure. Ah, the luxury of it. At least Annette had gotten this part right.

"To a safe flight," Heidi Johnson, her seatmate, said, and they clicked glasses.

Everly sipped the bubbly and sighed. "Are you able to sleep on these long flights?" she asked her companion.

"Not a problem."

This was encouraging news. "I'm stressed about making this cruise." Everly hated the thought of arriving in Brazil half brain dead from fatigue.

Heidi leaned her head close to Everly. "I have a little helper that puts me right to sleep."

Everly was interested. "What is it?" she asked.

Digging inside her purse, Heidi held up a small bottle of sleep aids, saying, "I take one of these little jewels. They work every time."

"I've never taken a sleeping pill." It was a rare night that Everly couldn't sleep.

"These knock me out in nothing flat and I sleep like a baby. By the time we land, I'm as fresh as a daisy."

Everly wished she'd thought ahead enough to have considered a sleeping pill. With so little time to get ready, she'd scrambled to pack, buy what she needed as best she could, and get to the airport in time for her flight. She felt breathless remembering rushing around her condo, grabbing clothes and stuffing everything in a lone suitcase. She did manage to pick up sunscreen and a few other necessities, but that was it. Never had she felt more ill prepared. Heaving a sigh, she told herself it would all work out in the end.

"The seats make up into a reasonably comfortable bed," Heidi told her. "Would you like one of my pills?"

"I would. Thanks." If Everly was going to arrive in Manaus with a functioning brain, sleep would certainly be helpful. Besides, what was she going to do with herself for the next ten hours if she couldn't sleep?

Her newfound friend handed over the small pill, which

Everly downed with the remainder of her champagne. When the attendant came to collect her dinner order, she ordered the pasta, which was surprisingly tasty, along with another glass of wine. By the time her dinner tray was removed, she was yawning. The sleeping aid had done its job in quick order, and Everly was grateful. She thanked Heidi again.

With the help of the flight attendant, Everly lowered her seat to the reclining position, laid her head down on the soft pillow, and closed her eyes. The lights in the cabin dimmed. Almost immediately she could feel herself drift off into the wonderful land of dreams.

Soon her head was whirling with the most fanciful visions, to the point that she was unsure if she was asleep or awake. She sighed as she saw herself walking along a sandy beach in her bikini with a full-length sheer cover-up blowing behind her in the wind. The warm, gentle waves of the Brazilian waters rippled against her bare feet as her footsteps left indentations in the wet sand. Admiring looks from other sun worshippers came her way as the wind tossed her soft brown hair about her face. With her head tilted toward the sun, she basked in the approving glow of admiration.

At five ten, she was the tallest of the three Lancaster girls. As a kid she was all legs. Her height had helped her in the business world, she felt, and she used it to her advantage, often wearing three- and four-inch heels. No man was going to intimidate her. She wore her thick shoulder-length hair straight, often securing it at her nape.

She wasn't looking for a relationship for the simple reason she didn't have time for one. Driven as she was to make Easy Home a success, she found her workweek frequently included twelve-hour days and often exceeded sixty hours a week. She was the first to arrive in the mornings and the last to leave. Her role in the company had taken over her life. Jack was right: She was stressed. What Everly needed was a life, a real life that involved relationships, laughter, and social events. All of which were sadly lacking. She couldn't even remember the last time she'd been on a date. Well, actually, she could. It was the night Dave broke up with her, claiming she was married to her job.

A vacation, she reasoned, in her half-dreamlike state, would be the perfect time for a romantic fling. A smile curved the edges of her mouth as she contemplated meeting the man of her dreams.

A fiery Latin lover. Ooh la la.

The cruise should give her ample opportunity to meet men. It was sure to be a romantically rich environment. Everly's dream was getting better by the minute. She pictured herself in the arms of a dashing man worthy of being a cover model. His muscles bulged as he bent her backward for a toe-curling kiss, sweeping her off her feet.

And then the lights came on.

Everly blinked against the brightness and pushed the button that would raise her bed into a sitting position. Rubbing her eyes, she heard the pilot announce that the plane would be landing in São Paulo within the next hour.

No sooner had she finished speaking when the flight attendant came down the aisle with a cart, offering coffee.

Everly continued to blink. It felt as if she were caught in a thick fog and was drifting outside her body.

Placing her hands over her face, she shook her head to clear her vision and wake up. It astonished her to learn she'd been asleep for nearly eight hours. It hadn't felt as if any time had passed at all. The last thing she remembered was her romantic fling with a Latin lover.

The flight attendant handed her a hot cup of coffee, which she eagerly downed, hoping that would help clear her head. She stared into the brew after each sip, as if the cup contained the answers to the universe and the solar system.

Her seatmate must have noticed her difficulty. "Are you having trouble waking up?"

"I . . . I don't know. I have the funniest feeling . . . like I'm in the middle . . . of a sandstorm." It sounded as if someone else was speaking. Everly hoped she wasn't slurring her words and feared she had.

The woman laughed lightly, as if she found the situation humorous.

Everly looked at Heidi, but it wasn't the same Heidi she'd

spent the first part of the flight with. This woman resembled a demonic creature who was laughing maniacally, as if Everly had sold her soul by swallowing that pill. She blinked and shook her head again and the original Heidi reappeared. Sighing with relief, she sagged against the back of the seat.

"Didn't I tell you these pills work every time?"

"You did." Everly kept her gaze straight forward, for fear Heidi would return to the unearthly creature from earlier.

"You've got to love drugs," Heidi said.

Horrified at what she might have digested, Everly swiveled her head to look at the other woman and asked in a slurred voice, "What . . . did you . . . give me?"

"Nothing illegal, just a normal sleeping pill. It hits people funny sometimes. No worries, it will all wear off in a few hours."

The flight attendant came by and collected the coffee mug and the plane was readied for landing. The Boeing 767 took a hard bounce against the tarmac and eventually coasted to the Jetway.

Although she continued to feel like she was having an out-of-body experience, Everly exited the plane. She staggered a few steps, as if she'd been on a drinking binge, and nearly lost her balance. Perhaps it was mixing the sleeping pill with the alcohol that was responsible for this side effect.

Once in the airport, she needed to get through customs and find the gate to her connecting flight to Manaus. She'd never heard of the city, which was clearly somewhere on the coast. People were talking around her and it was the oddest thing. Their words made no sense. It was as if the letters had stacked themselves on top of one another like building blocks. Even though she strained to make sense of what was being said, she couldn't understand a word, until she realized no one was speaking English.

She was punch-drunk, hardly able to remain upright and unable to understand a word anyone said to her. Fumbling in her purse, she reached for her boarding pass and realized that because of her missed flights, not only was she changing planes, she was changing airlines as well. Stymied, she froze, completely overwhelmed, unsure what to do.

As if an answer to prayer, a man pushing an empty wheelchair rolled past her. Frantically she waved her arm until she got his attention. Without help she didn't have a snowball's chance of making this flight, let alone the cruise.

Before he could object, she awkwardly fell into the chair and handed him her boarding pass. Once he had it, she thrust her arm straight out and shouted, "Forward."

Good thing she did, because the gate was a good half-mile from where she'd cleared customs. Her head continued to whirl around as if she were caught up in a tornado, and she clenched her purse like it was Toto. Only she wasn't in Kansas, although it felt like she'd landed somewhere over the rainbow.

Wheeling past one gate after another, Everly continued to blink, hoping that would help to clear her vision. The connection was tight, and if not for the ride, it was unlikely she would have made the flight on time.

It helped that she was in business class. She was even more grateful when the flight attendant greeted her in English. "Is there anything I can get you?" he asked.

"Coffee, please."

Within a few minutes he returned with a fresh cup of coffee.

Grateful, Everly drank it with the hope it would help clear her head. "We're going to Manaus, correct?" The last thing she needed was to board the wrong flight.

"That's right."

"I've never heard of this city." World geography wasn't her strong suit.

"Really? It's famous."

"It's fairly large, then."

"Oh yes, I think the population is well over two million."

"Really?" That was a surprise. For the last six years, her focus was on real estate. She could name nearly every county of Illinois. But ask her to point out Liechtenstein on a map and she was clueless.

The attendant had to move on to ready the plane for departure, cutting off their brief conversation.

Just when everything seemed to be coming together

there was a problem with the airplane, and they were delayed thirty minutes, which cut the time to make the cruise even tighter. Everly couldn't think about it. If she missed the cruise, then so be it. Even though she was nervous, she quickly fell asleep and woke as it was announced that they were about to depart on the four-hour flight to Manaus. She could fret or she could sleep. Sleep chose her. Leaning her head back, Everly slipped into dreamland as if she hadn't a care in the world. This must be the way Jack felt all the time, carefree. Lighthearted, with a devil-may-care attitude.

By the time the plane landed she was almost back to normal. Checking the time, she saw that she had twenty minutes left of her three-hour leeway. Rushing to baggage claim, she got her suitcase and shot out of the terminal to catch a cab.

It took her five tries before she found a driver who was relatively fluent in English. "I need to get to the cruise dock, pronto." She read off the name of the pier from her travel document. "The ship is waiting for me . . . at least I hope it is. I'll give you double your normal fare if you get me there quickly." She swatted at the mosquito buzzing around in the cab's interior.

The words hadn't left her lips when the driver pulled away from the curb, wheels screeching, leaving rubber behind. Everly tumbled across the seat when he made a wild turn. Once she righted herself, she grabbed hold of the seatbelt and tried unsuccessfully to lock it into place. The mosquito wasn't helping matters any. The pesky fellow wouldn't leave her alone.

"Your first time Manaus?" he asked as he sped through a red light.

Hanging on to the seat in front of her with both hands, Everly nodded. "First time."

"You not see opera house?"

"You have an opera house?"

"Very famous."

"Perhaps another time," she said, as she slid all the way across the backseat as he took another crazy turn. It felt as if the vehicle had gone up on two wheels. Everly let out a cry of alarm, which didn't seem to concern the driver.

"Come see fish market, too."

"Okay. Sure." Not in this lifetime. Everly intensely disliked the smell of dead fish.

"Where you from in America?" he asked.

"Chicago."

How he was able to drive like he was Vin Diesel in The Fast and the Furious and carry on a conversation baffled Everly.

"I've got cousins in Chicago."

"Have you been there?"

"No, only California in Cabo San Lucas."

"That's Mexico."

Taking his eyes off the road, he swiveled his head around to look at her. "You sure?"

"Yes, quite sure."

"Funny, my cousin doesn't think so."

"Is this the same cousin in Chicago?"

"No different cousin."

Everly noticed they were in an industrial area of the city. Soon afterward, the cabbie slammed on his brake so hard, she was nearly catapulted over the seat next to the driver. Breathing as hard as if she'd completed a marathon, she reached inside her purse and handed her driver a fistful of money. He beamed her a smile and helped her out of the car. Grabbing her suitcase, he held on to her elbow as they speed-walked to the gangway.

A man was standing just inside the ship. "Are you Daisy Lancaster?" he shouted.

Hearing her given name gave her pause. Naturally the ship would have the same name that was on her passport. "Yes," she shouted back.

"Good." He held out his arm and helped her up the last few steps. "Welcome aboard," he said. "Glad you made it."

The cabbie handed off her suitcase to the ship's steward. He took it and smiled approvingly at Everly. "I have always appreciated a woman who could pack light."

She smiled dryly. "Am I the last one to board?"

"You are." He reached for a phone and issued instructions to the crew before he said, "I'll escort you to your stateroom."

"Thank you." That was kind of him, and she dutifully followed him to the elevator. As they exited, she heard the ship's horn as the vessel prepared to leave the dock. Because of the rush, she hadn't paid much notice to the ship itself. Now that she was aboard, it was much smaller than what she'd anticipated.

Her stateroom wasn't anything to brag about, either. She stood in the doorway, shocked at how utilitarian it was. A bed and a nightstand and a door that led to the bathroom. There was a small desk with a chair, too. "This is my room?" she asked, doing her best to hide her dismay.

"Yes, top deck. You were lucky to get it, as we had a last-minute cancellation."

Everly remembered Annette excitedly explaining that she was fortunate to have found a ship with space at this late date.

"Do you have my room key?" she asked.

The steward met her gaze. "There are no locks on the stateroom doors."

"No locks?" she repeated, certain she hadn't heard him correctly.

"That's correct. None of the staterooms have locks."

Looking around, she noticed several other standard items one would expect were missing as well. "No phones?"

"No."

"Television?"

"None of those, either."

"In any of the staterooms?"

"That's correct."

A cold feeling settled over her, chilling her to the bone. She held her breath and then asked the one question that was a matter of life or death. "What about Internet access?"

"Afraid not."

Horrified, Everly sank onto the bed. "I need the Internet."

"I'm sorry, Miss, the answers to all your questions are in the brochure, including the fact there's no Internet while on board."

What brochure? Annette seemed to have conveniently forgotten to include that. "You don't understand. I can't function without the Internet." She would need to speak to the captain immediately. "What kind of luxury cruise is this?"

"Luxury cruise?" he repeated, shaking his head. "Lady, this is the Amazon Explorer."

Everly blinked, certain she hadn't heard him correctly. "Are you telling me I'm on a cruise going down the Amazon River?"

"That's exactly what I'm telling you."

CHAPTER THREE

"I need to speak to the captain," Everly said, hoping her voice displayed the proper amount of urgency.

"Miss, Captain Martin is busy navigating. He can't be bothered."

"You don't understand, this is a matter of great importance. I need to get off this ship."

"The best I can do is have you speak to the purser."

Leaping back to her feet, she said, "Then please take me to him."

The young steward looked pale, as if he feared he'd be tossed overboard by doing as she asked. "Yes, Miss."

Everly had to find a way to get this ship to turn back around, and the sooner she spoke with someone in authority, the better.

She followed the steward down the narrow hallway to an office. Two men were inside making small talk. The man she had to assume was the purser looked up when she entered the room. He looked to the steward for an explanation.

"Ms. Lancaster asked to speak with you right away," he said, and quickly extricated himself from the small room.

"I'm Alex Freeman," he said, and extended his hand. "And this is Asher Adams; he's the naturalist on board."

She stepped forward and shook hands with both men. "Daisy Lancaster." She didn't want to confuse him with a name other than what was on the manifest.

"How can I help you, Daisy?"

"There's been an unfortunate mistake. I need to get off this cruise ship."

Both men stared at her blankly, as if she'd spoken in Latin.

Alex shook his head. "What's the problem?" he asked.

Rather than go into details about Annette having finessed Everly into this ridiculous cruise down the Amazon, she tried to explain.

"I need access to the Internet."

"There isn't any, which is stated—"

"In the brochure," she completed for him, "only I didn't get the brochure."

"That is unfortunate. I apologize, but there's nothing I can do for your situation."

Everly tried again. "In simple terms, the Internet is vital to my being in touch with my business."

"I'm sorry," Alex said, "but—"

"You don't understand. I will die without the Internet. I can live without a television or even a room phone. My only two requirements are the Internet and something that will go flush in the night." She hadn't checked the bathroom to see if there was even a toilet.

"The toilets work amazingly well," the naturalist said, as if finding this conversation amusing.

Everly glared at him. "It might be best if I speak to the captain."

"I'm afraid he's currently occupied with his duties and can't be disturbed."

"This is an emergency," she said, seeing that neither man was taking her seriously. "I have to get off this ship."

"Unfortunately, at this point that is impossible."

Everly dropped her head as frustration overwhelmed her. Time to try another tactic. "Okay, let's be creative here. How far is it to the next port?"

The two men shared a look as if she'd lost her mind.

"Come on, guys," she encouraged, "work with me. Perhaps there is a way the captain could arrange for me to be picked up and taken to the nearest airport at the first stop."

Both men frowned. "What you don't understand," Alex Freeman said, "is that there are no cities of consequence on the itinerary."

"You're right, I don't understand. What are you saying?"

It was Asher Adams who explained. "This is a two-week

cruise down the Amazon River. There's nothing but rainforest. There isn't anything even resembling a port or an airfield. Bottom line, you won't be able to leave the ship now that we've departed Manaus."

For a moment Everly was too stunned to speak. "You've got to be kidding me."

Asher's look was sympathetic. "Sorry, no."

Everly let the information soak in. "Perhaps if I offer to pay for any expense the captain would incur, he might be willing to reconsider."

Asher shook his head. "I'll be happy to get the captain when he's available, but I can assure you it's highly unlikely. Returning to port would have to be scheduled well in advance with the port authorities. The expense would be tens of thousands of dollars."

She'd had to make one final attempt.

"I'm sorry we can't be more accommodating, Daisy," Asher added.

Defeated, Everly slumped her shoulders. Annette had gotten her revenge in spades.

"If you're willing to put aside your disappointment and give this cruise a chance, I believe you'll fall in love with the rainforest," the naturalist added. "You might come away with a deep appreciation of your time aboard the Amazon Explorer."

That didn't seem possible. Unsure what other options she

had, Everly returned to her stateroom. Sitting on the end of her bed, she covered her face with her hands and decided she had no choice but to make the best of this situation. The naturalist was right. If she let go of her expectations, she might actually enjoy herself. Or at least be less miserable.

Everly went ahead and unpacked the few items inside her suitcase before jumping in the shower. She did her best thinking in the shower. Soaking away the tension from a full day at the office was often the first thing she did once she arrived back at her condo. If ever she needed stress relief, it was now.

She let the hot water rain down on her in the cramped space as she considered how best to deal with this unfortunate situation.

Rather than let her anger get the best of her, Everly planned to take matters into her own hands. One way or another, she'd make the most of this. Once she was able to speak with the captain, perhaps he'd come up with a creative solution. Surely there was a way to get her back to civilization.

She was barely out of the shower when a mandatory fire drill was announced over the loudspeaker. Quickly dressing in white linen pants and a navy-blue silk blouse, Everly searched her closet for the life vest.

As it turned out, the meeting location was on the same deck as her stateroom. Everly carried her life vest down the passageway to the gathering area. One step into the room and she realized she was completely out of her element. Every other passenger was dressed as if ready to explore the jungle, or in this case, the rainforest. The wardrobe of choice was beige pants with multiple pockets, a matching long-sleeved shirt, hiking boots, and a large oversized hat.

Everly was the immediate center of attention. Smiling weakly, she entered the room and was handed a badge to hang around her neck with her nametag.

Both the purser and the naturalist were with the group. She felt Asher studying her. He looked to be in his mid-thirties and was of average build, but muscular, and she intuitively knew he didn't get his bulk in any gym. He was deeply tanned and had warm brown eyes and an easy smile. His coffee-colored hair appeared to have a habit of falling over one side of his brow. She had to admit he was kind of cute.

He walked over to her and smiled. "I hope you took my words to heart."

"I did," she said, even though she was still hoping to find a solution. If not, she would have to make the most of this adventure.

The fire drill took only a few minutes and was led by the safety officer, Mike Hanes. Once it was finished, Asher was introduced. He stepped before those gathered in the room.

"As Mike said, I'm a naturalist. You are in for an exciting two weeks. I'll be giving several talks, familiarizing you with some of the wide variety of plants and wildlife you can expect to see. You're going to come away with a full appreciation for the beauty of this rainforest. My sole purpose is to make this one of the most memorable trips of your life." Having said this, Asher introduced the rest of the crew, including a photographer, the chef, and other key members. At the end of his talk, the captain welcomed everyone himself and explained that he would soon be needed on the bridge. "I didn't want to let this opportunity pass to welcome you myself. Now, if you'll excuse me."

A polite applause followed. Asher came to the forefront once more. "Thank you, Captain. I want to remind everyone that there will be an informal social gathering in thirty minutes. Afterward I'll review our itinerary and some of the exciting adventures we have planned over the next two weeks."

Trying to be as unobtrusive as possible, Everly followed the captain into the passageway. "Captain Martin," she said, stopping him. "If you have a few minutes, I have an urgent request."

"You're Ms. Lancaster?"

"Yes, that's me." Her reputation had apparently preceded her.

"I've already spoken to Alex. Regretfully, there's nothing to be done. Now, if you'll excuse me."

Defeated, Everly nodded. If she continued to pressure the crew they would look upon her as a pest. She returned to her room. As she replaced the life vest in the minuscule closet, she noticed a mosquito bite on her arm. It could only have happened in the taxi during her ride to the dock. The skin surrounding the red bump burned to the touch and it already itched something fierce. She had been distracted earlier, but now the bite was front and center.

In the social hour that followed, she learned that this afternoon gathering would take place daily. The passengers and staff would review the highlights of the day with wine and small appetizers before going in for the evening meal. She quickly picked up on the fact that everyone was friendly and eager to share something about themselves. Within the first half-hour, Everly met two college professors, a psychiatrist, a chemist, several other professionals, and a friendly retired couple from Germany. She was surprised to discover there were only forty passengers along with thirty crew members.

Her two favorites were a long-married couple, the Browns, who were celebrating their forty-fifth wedding anniversary with the cruise.

"This has long been on David's bucket list," Janice said.

"What about your bucket list?" Everly asked, thinking it must have been a sacrifice for Janice to agree to a trip on the Amazon.

"Oh, I've had my springtime in Paris. It was David's turn to choose where we headed off to next. I wasn't sure at first, but the more I read up about Brazil and the rainforest, the more enthused I became. I think we're both going to enjoy every minute of these two weeks."

Everly could only hope she would as well, although it was highly doubtful. The irritation on her arm was at the point of being painful; the sting was getting harder to ignore. She'd never had a reaction to a mosquito bite before and wondered if this was a different breed of insect than what she was accustomed to in Indiana, where she'd been raised.

As she moved about the room, chatting with the other passengers, she learned that nearly everyone on board had taken one or more of these explorer adventures. One couple spoke of their trip to Antarctica. Another mentioned being in the Galápagos Islands. There were trips down the Nile and adventures in Iceland. It seemed every other passenger on board was a seasoned traveler. Working the hours she did, Everly had rarely left the States.

After an hour of socializing, the purser had everyone take a seat as he reviewed the itinerary. The route was displayed on a large television screen. The first week entailed making headway down the river. At some point they would turn around and return to Manaus. As she reviewed the map, Everly noticed that what Alex had told her earlier was true. The entire voyage was made up of rainforest and jungle.

"I hope you've all read the brochure that came as part of your packet. In case you haven't had a chance to review it, the one point I need to reiterate is the environmental policies that don't allow us to take water from the Amazon. That means water usage will be held at a strict limit while we are on the river. We ask that passengers only take two showers a week."

Everly gasped. She'd already taken one of her allotted showers.

"Is that a problem, Daisy?" Alex asked.

Unwilling to stand out more than she already did, Everly shook her head. "Not in the least. It came as a surprise is all."

Seeing that she hadn't read the brochure, she hadn't received the list of wardrobe suggestions, either, if looking at the others was any indication. Annette had a lot to answer for, and Everly fully intended to make sure she did.

"Tomorrow morning will be the first of our lectures from Asher Adams," Alex said. "I know you'll enjoy what he has to say. He'll be giving us a general review of what we can expect once we're in the Zodiacs and on the Amazon itself."

Other than what she'd learned being raised on the farm, Everly had never taken much notice of flora and fauna.

"In the next few days we'll be taking the Zodiacs out every day. I'm pleased to share that in the second week of our exploration of the Amazon, we have the opportunity to meet with a group of indigenous people. We'll venture into the rainforest itself to their small village and share a traditional meal prepared especially for us."

This was apparently a surprise, as the others responded with excited chatter. No way was Everly going to be getting into a Zodiac and walking through the rainforest in linen pants and a silk blouse. She hadn't come prepared for this type of adventure. When the time came, she'd be staying aboard. She could read the books she'd downloaded. Perhaps, if she was lucky, there might even be a small swimming pool. She'd find ways to amuse herself until she could return to Chicago and seek out her own revenge. Annette would pay for this.

Dinner followed and Everly made her way into the compact dining area. There was no assigned seating and she was tempted to skip, seeing that her arm itched something fierce from the mosquito bite. Just as she was about to excuse herself, Janice Brown invited her to join her and her husband. The exploration team followed behind and Alex and his wife chose to sit at a table with space for two.

Asher Adams stepped up to the table. "May I join you?" he asked the three of them.

"Of course," David said.

"Please," Janice confirmed. "It would be our honor."

Asher looked to Everly. "By all means," she concurred. She suspected he saw her as a troublemaker and wanted to curtail any discontent.

Asher pulled out the chair and sat next to her.

"How wonderful that we're going to be able to walk

through the rainforest," Janice said, as she passed the freshly baked bread to Everly. "I can't imagine we could have a better guide. We were with Asher in Antarctica," she explained to Everly.

As if he sensed her reluctance, Asher turned to Everly. "I hope you'll join us when we explore the rainforest."

"I'll see how I feel when the time comes," she said before sinking her teeth into the bread.

"Oh, you must!" Janice insisted. "You can't let this opportunity pass you by."

Everly knew she needed an attitude adjustment. It would take time, but she was determined to do her best. Turning to Asher, she asked, "There doesn't happen to be a swimming pool of any kind on board, is there?"

He looked surprised by the question. "Sorry, no."

"That's what I thought." Growing more uncomfortable by the moment, she squirmed in her chair. She debated on excusing herself and checking the bite again. It seemed to be getting worse.

"You will join us for the excursion, won't you?" Janice pressed.

"I'd like to," Everly said, unwilling to discourage the other woman's enthusiasm. "Unfortunately, I don't have anything to wear that's appropriate . . . there was a miscommunication and I didn't realize this was the cruise I'd booked."

"That's a shame," David added, sounding genuinely sorry.

"It is," Janice agreed. "I'd be happy to loan you a few of my clothes, but I fear you and I are nowhere near the same size."

"That's generous of you," Everly said, sincerely touched by the other woman's thoughtfulness. She rubbed at her upper arm; this bug bite was driving her insane. It ached as badly as it itched.

"You would be willing if you had the proper clothes, though?" Asher asked.

Her three dinner companions awaited her response. She didn't want to disappoint them, seeing that they each were anxious to include her.

"Of course, but as I said, I didn't pack anything suitable."

Janice turned her attention to Asher. "I'm anxious to hear your talk tomorrow morning."

"Thank you. The rainforest is bursting with life. Millions of species of plants and animals make their home here, along with several unique tribes. The group we'll be meeting are the Caribs."

"The Caribs," David repeated, nodding toward his wife.

"Yes, there are scattered remnants of ethnic groups with their own distinctive language and culture that remain in the tropical forests. At best estimate there are as many as seventy-seven groups living there with no contact with the outside world."

"That many?"

"The majority come from Brazil, with twelve to fifteen such groups in Peru. I've met several contacted groups over the course of my time. Virtually all have been affected by the outside world, although many men continue to wear traditional garb of loincloths and the women go topless. Some have chosen to dress in Western clothes, but the people we have the opportunity to meet have stayed true to their traditions."

"That's amazing in this day and age," Janice commented.

"You'd be surprised by how adaptable these people are to the world. Many use metal pots, pans, and utensils for everyday life. Some make handicrafts to sell to tourists and routinely venture into the city to bring food and wares to market. In Manaus, I was able to purchase a dart gun for my nephew, Morgan."

Janice laughed. "I bet he loved that."

"I haven't given it to him yet, but I plan to on my next trip to Chicago."

"Chicago?" Everly repeated, as she reached for a second dinner roll.

"Yes, my brother and his wife live there."

"Oh. That's where I live."

He smiled at her before returning his attention to the Browns.

"Are the indigenous people able to grow their own food,

or do they forage for it in the rainforest?" Everly asked as their dinner was served. Her father would be interested in that sort of information, seeing that he had worked the farm all of his adult life.

Asher continued the dinner conversation, giving them tidbits of information about the hunting and cultivation of crops. He spoke of how they grew rice and a variety of bananas while Everly listened as best she could. Her arm grew more uncomfortable by the minute, making it difficult to focus. She could hardly wait to get back to her room and check out the problem. She'd been bitten before, and while it was mildly irritating, it'd never affected her like this.

The meal was good, despite her discomfort, but then she hadn't eaten in more hours than she could remember.

Dinner was followed by an announcement that a movie would be showing, detailing life in the rainforest. Eager to return to her room and look at her arm, Everly decided to forgo the movie. From the conversation during the social hour, she learned that several of her fellow passengers had arrived a few days earlier and had adjusted to the time difference. The couple from Germany, who spoke excellent English, had arrived a full week earlier and had the opportunity to tour Manaus and Rio before boarding the Amazon Explorer.

The moment she returned to her stateroom, Everly peeled off her shirt and looked in the bathroom mirror. The bite that had been a small red bump before dinner had grown to the size of a bread plate, covering nearly her entire upper arm.

Everly bit into her lower lip, unsure what to do. It was clear she was having an intense allergic reaction to the bite. She'd been in her room only a short time when there was a knock on her door. Remembering that there were no locks, she didn't risk not answering. She quickly buttoned up her blouse.

"Yes?" she said, opening her door.

Asher stood in the passageway outside. "I've come to check to see if you're all right. I noticed you seemed uncomfortable at dinner."

Everly's head started to swim. "I'm okay," she said. "Really, it's nothing."

"Are you sure?"

"Oh yes, I'm quite sure," she said, right before she slumped forward into his arms in a dead faint.

CHAPTER FOUR

Everly woke to find herself on top of her bed with Asher Adams looking down on her. She blinked several times, wondering how she'd gotten from the door to her bed.

"You fainted," Asher announced.

Rising on one elbow, Everly blinked at him several times. "I fainted?" She shook her head, finding that impossible to believe. "Must be an adverse reaction to the sleeping pill I took on my flight here."

He frowned as if he wasn't inclined to believe her. "I doubt a sleeping pill would cause you to faint."

"Or it could be the mosquito bite I got on the ride between the airport and the ship."

"Would you mind if I took a look?" Asher asked. "I have some advanced training and the captain calls upon me when there's a medical issue."

"I suppose that would be all right." She sat up and unbuttoned her blouse enough to free her arm. "It feels hot and itches like crazy."

Asher gently held her arm. "Have you ever had a reaction to a mosquito bite before?"

"No. I was raised on a farm and was bitten a hundred times. I've never had anything like this happen."

Asher carefully examined the bite, and Everly had to admit the redness and swelling around the area were impressive. It had spread to the entire upper part of her arm. "The mosquitoes in the Amazon carry a number of different viruses."

"Will you need to amputate?" she asked, mainly to lighten the mood, seeing how serious Asher looked.

Asher didn't even crack a smile. "Some of these viruses can be serious, Daisy. How are you feeling generally?"

"What do you mean?"

"Headache? Nauseated?"

Now that he mentioned it, she could feel a humdinger of a headache approaching. "I think if I get a good night's sleep, I'll be fine by morning."

"I'll check in with you then," Asher said. "But first I'm going to get you something to take down the swelling and help you rest comfortably."

"Not another sleeping pill." This time she wasn't joking. She appreciated his concern, but she had a tough constitution. The bite didn't overly worry her. She had malaria pills and had gotten the required shots, so she should be fine. A tiny mosquito bite wasn't going to do her in.

"No sleeping pill," he promised.

Asher left and returned a few minutes later with two capsules. He explained what they were and how they would help before she swallowed them down.

Not long afterward, Everly fell asleep. It was hard to believe that less than twenty-four hours earlier she'd been in Chicago in the middle of a blizzard. She woke in the middle of the night with her stomach roiling. Her head pounded and she felt dizzy as she rushed into her bathroom. She arrived in the nick of time to empty the contents of her stomach. With her hand pressed against her midsection, she stumbled back to bed. She felt wretched, worse than she had in years.

At eight the following morning when she was a no-show for breakfast, there was a knock against her door.

"Daisy, it's Asher."

"Come in," she called, her voice weak.

The instant he stepped into the room she saw his eyes darken with anxiety. She felt certain she was burning up with fever, and her head pounded like someone with evil intent had taken residence inside her.

"You don't look any better," he said, coming to sit on the side of her mattress. He pressed his hand against her forehead. "You're feverish."

Everly felt like she was about to burst into tears. Her bottom lip quivered. So much for a robust constitution. This was worse than anything she could remember; she wanted her mother and Mom's homemade chicken soup.

"Everything hurts," she whispered, leaning back against her pillow. "My hair hurts. My teeth hurt. My fingernails are throbbing."

"I guess you were serious," he said, grinning.

"What?"

"You really will die without the Internet."

"Very funny," she grumbled. "How long is this reaction thing going to last?"

Asher pulled the chair up next to her bed and sat. "Some people don't feel sick or suffer any symptoms."

"Not what I wanted to hear."

His eyes were sympathetic. "You should be right as rain in five to seven days."

Everly flopped back against her pillow. "That long?" She couldn't imagine feeling like this for an entire week. Covering her face with both hands, she groaned aloud.

Asher left only to return a few minutes later with more medication and liquids. He sat with her until she drank it all down. By this point, Everly was feeling beyond being heroic. She sniffled several times and reached for a tissue at her bedside, loudly blowing her nose. The drugs Asher had given her seemed to make her woozy and talkative at the same time.

"I'm stronger than this," she insisted. It felt as if everything had gone downhill with the speed of an Olympic skier since she'd left Chicago. "I refuse to let a little mosquito bring me down." To prove her point, she raised her index finger to the ceiling and announced, "I. Have. Milked. Cows."

Asher gently squeezed her hand. "You'll feel better soon," he promised.

"I'm not a weak person," she repeated, finding it vital that he know she wasn't a sniveling complainer. "Have you been chased by a hen who doesn't want to give up her eggs?"

"I can't say that I have."

That seemed to satisfy her sense of righteousness. "Well, I have, and I'm here to tell you I've had to stand up for myself first with those hens and then in school and also in my business. There's not a lot I can't do when I put my mind to it. I am not about to let a tiny mosquito take me out."

"I believe you." If he found her tirade amusing, he didn't let on.

"I think I can sleep now." She lay back and closed her eyes as blissful slumber overtook her.

When Everly woke, she saw that Asher had remained at her side. He had a cool cloth on her forehead and smiled down on her. "You're awake."

"How long did I sleep?"

"A couple of hours."

"You stayed with me all that time?"

"Off and on," he said. "You're looking better. How do you feel?"

Everly had to think about it before she nodded. "My head isn't pounding as hard as earlier."

"I brought you in some soup. Try it and see how it rests in your stomach."

Sitting up in bed, Everly leaned forward as Asher adjusted her pillows. "So you're a farm girl."

"I was raised on a farm. I live and work in the city now."

"That's a big change."

"Yup, couldn't get away from it fast enough. Don't get me wrong. I love my family, they're the best, but I much prefer life in the city." She sipped the apple juice he'd brought her. "I miss them from time to time. You can't imagine how crazy it gets when we're all together."

"You come from a large family?"

She nodded. "Rose and Lily are my sisters."

"And you're Daisy."

"Mom and Dad had a theme going and they weren't about to stop with me. My brothers are Jeff and John. They're identical twins and work with my dad on the farm. One generation to the next."

"And your sisters?"

"They're both married, raising families." Talking about her family made Everly yearn to be with them all again, and at the same time she felt the familiar anxiety about fitting in when she was vastly different from her siblings. She'd balked at taking the entire month off, but even a few days away from the office and her thinking was starting to change. Perhaps it was being sick and wanting her mother's special soup.

"What about you?"

"There's just my brother and me. Daniel is a heart surgeon in Chicago. He's married and has a couple of kids. Mom and Dad both were in academia and have retired in Arizona."

"You're not married?" Everly hoped she wasn't being obvious.

"No. I've been with the Explorer group for several years and it suits me. I'm something of an introvert, although when it comes to talking about nature, I'm not the least bit shy." He scooted a chair closer to her bed. "As for dating and such, most of the passengers who book the Explorer cruises are retired, looking for a unique learning experience, so there isn't much opportunity to meet women my age."

"Oh . . . I can understand that." Everly's one semiserious relationship since college had ended abruptly and painfully. "I'm so busy in my job that I haven't had much time to date myself."

He cocked his eyebrows. "Why's that? You're an attractive woman; I'm sure the men of Chicago aren't blind."

"Thanks," she said and shrugged. "The thing is, after graduation, I worked with a start-up company. It was an intense, exciting time getting this online real estate company off the ground. I've had my head buried in work for so long I sort of abandoned my social life." She didn't mention how Jack had let her take over more and more of the business aspects because she was better suited in that area. He was the charmer, the schmoozer, and so likable it was hard to find fault with him.

"And you enjoy that?" He made it sound as if he found her dedication to her work difficult to understand.

"As much as you enjoy being a naturalist," she returned.

Asher grinned. "Touché. I'm not much of a big-city guy myself. All that traffic and noise. I was never one for crowds. I crave silence. Most people are so intent on getting where they're going, they miss out on the best parts of life."

Everly mulled over his words and understood what he was saying. "I can see that, but at the same time, there's an energy to the city, a rhythm, a beat that feeds my soul. I thrive on it."

They talked for a bit longer before Asher was scheduled to give another nature talk. She learned that his interest in nature started with an ant farm he got for Christmas when he was six years old. From that point forward he devoured everything he could find on the subject. Everly found it easy to talk to him.

Everly didn't see him again until late in the afternoon when he returned with a dinner plate. She was feeling slightly better, but the sight of food almost made her gag. It was back to broth and other liquids for a second day.

"How are you doing?" he asked on day three.

"A tad bit better."

He set the food tray down on her nightstand and she sat up, bracing her back against the pillows.

When Asher started to leave, she stopped him. "Would you mind staying for a few minutes?" She hated to admit how bored she was, and how eager she was for his company.

"Sure," he said, "but I don't want your dinner to grow cold."

"I'm not hungry. I'll eat it later."

Asher scooted the chair closer to the bed. They'd talked a lot the last few days, but they never seemed to lack for conversation.

"Do you want to play three questions?" he asked. This was a silly game they had made up, taking turns asking each other three questions.

Everly had enjoyed getting to know him and found him good company. "I do," she said, warming to the idea. She'd spent part of the afternoon formulating the questions.

"You go first," he said, gesturing to her.

She snuggled against the pillows. "Who was your first kiss? And how old were you?"

Asher grinned. "That's two questions."

She smiled and rolled her eyes. "Whatever."

"My first kiss was Mary Lou Chavez. I was thirteen and my best friend dared me to kiss her and so I did."

"Did you like her?"

"You're using up your turn mighty fast. Are you sure you want to squander your third question on something so trivial?" Leaning back in his chair, he crossed his arms, a smile at the edges of his mouth.

"Maybe."

"Since you asked, I'll tell you. I thought Mary Lou was cute, but our kiss was a disaster because our braces locked."

It hurt to laugh, but Everly couldn't hold back. "You won the bet, though."

"I did, but my father was furious with me when Mary Lou's father insisted I pay the dentist bill since the wires in her braces got twisted. My allowance couldn't cover it, so Dad ended up having to pay it for me. I might have won the bet, but it took me three months of taking on odd jobs to reimburse my dad."

In sympathy, Everly patted his knee. "The course of true love is never smooth," she said.

"Truer words were never spoken. Okay, my turn." He leaned forward and studied her for a moment. "What was the last book you read?"

"It was a historical romance by one of my favorite authors."

His eyes widened as if surprised. "You read romance?"

She laughed. "Are you sure you want to waste a second question?"

"No, you're right. Forget I asked that, but it surprises me."

"Why?"

"You don't seem the type to indulge in that genre, sharp business executive that you are."

"Really? And what type is that?"

He looked uneasy, as if he'd said something he shouldn't. "I don't know. I've always thought of those books as sappy and unrealistic."

"Then you'd be wrong. They're positive and uplifting and give me hope of finding my own handsome hero one day."

"Ah, that leads to my next question. What qualities do you look for in a hero?"

Everly tilted her head to one side and mulled over her answer. "I know I mentioned handsome, but that isn't really a quality, because beauty is only skin-deep. It's superficial. What matters is the heart of a person. Their values and priorities. My perfect hero is a man who knows himself, who cares about the world and the environment, who is connected to family, and who loves God and will love me. He has to have a good sense of humor and be willing to laugh at himself."

Asher nodded as if he approved.

"It might sound silly, but I'd like for him to be handy around the house, too. My dad is like that. I doubt there is anything my dad can't fix. But he's intelligent enough to know when he can't and call in a professional."

"Sounds like a smart man."

"He is," Everly agreed, realizing anew how much she appreciated her dad. When describing her perfect hero, she felt a gnawing ache in her heart, recognizing how far off-kilter her life had become. When she'd left for this cruise her head had been full of doubt that Easy Home would survive without her. Here she was, stuck on the Amazon with no way to connect with her team, and she survived. What was happening back in Chicago took on less and less importance. It'd taken these days in bed, when all she had to do was think, to realize how distorted her life had become. The need to be needed had led her down a path she never intended to take.

"You have another question left," she reminded him.

He seemed deep in thought. "Do you think you'll feel well enough to take a walk a little later?"

That was his question? She'd expected something more along the line of the others. She wondered at his mood but didn't question him.

"Yes, I think so." She'd been out of bed for brief periods of time out of necessity. The light-headedness had gotten better and she didn't feel nearly as weak as she had the first couple days.

"Then I'll return later."

The mood had shifted and Everly wasn't sure what had happened. They'd been teasing and joking, and all at once Asher had grown serious. What was that about?

CHAPTER FIVE

Asher left Daisy and paused outside her stateroom, his thoughts whirling around in his head like a vortex. He hated that she'd had such a harsh reaction to the mosquito bite and was happy to be the one assigned to look after her.

It was rare for him to have this amount of quality time with any one passenger. He found himself looking forward to mealtimes so he could spend a few extra minutes with Daisy. He still smiled over her comment that she'd milked cows and her insistence that she was strong and capable. After being with her, he didn't doubt what she'd said was true.

He wasn't sure how they'd come up with the idea of this game of asking each other three questions. He found her easy company and was curious about her and her life. He'd learned a lot about her childhood on the farm and how hard she'd worked to get this online real estate company to be the success that it was. He admired her grit and her business savvy. She told him early on that she'd changed her name to Everly.

Everly?

He preferred Daisy. To him she would always be Daisy.

Everything had gone well until he'd made the mistake of asking her to describe her perfect hero. Asher wasn't sure what he'd expected. He assumed her opinion would be shaped by the romance novels she read, and half expected her to say the man of her dreams had to be tall, dark, and handsome.

Instead, she'd unwittingly described him to a tee.

Asher knew himself and he cared about the environment. He had a strong connection with his family and was a believer, having been raised in faith. He was an introvert, but he had a good sense of humor. And he didn't have a problem laughing at himself. Plus, he was handy. Give him pliers and a roll of duct tape and he could jerry-rig just about anything. Daisy couldn't possibly have known that.

What shook him even more than her description of what she was looking for in a man was how perfectly she fit into his own version of the woman he would seek to share his life with. If circumstances were different, he could easily see himself falling for Daisy.

Circumstances weren't different, though.

Daisy had spoken enthusiastically of her life in the city and how much she thrived there. Life on the farm had never suited her. Her older sisters had married young and never left, choosing instead to raise families in small-town America. From her early teens, Daisy had made the decision to get her college degree and work in the business world. Her drive had made Easy Home a huge success.

An ambitious woman like Daisy would never be happy with the life that was most comfortable to him. They were from different worlds and never the twain shall meet.

As promised, Asher collected Daisy to take a walk. He found her dressed and sitting on the edge of the bed, waiting for him. A weak smile lit up her face when he entered her stateroom.

"Are you sure you feel up to this?" he asked, noticing how pale she was. The last thing he wanted was for her to overdo it.

"I'm tired of being trapped in this room. I'll have you escort me back if it's too much for me."

Now that he saw her, he wasn't convinced this was the best idea. "I'm holding you to that."

Asher helped her stand, keeping an arm around her waist. It took a bit for her to get stable on her feet. "How dizzy are you?"

"Only a little."

He wasn't sure he believed her. "Remember, if it's too much, you need to say something."

"I will."

They walked to the meeting area and then turned back before they entered the room. Asher didn't think Daisy would appreciate anyone seeing her in this weakened condition.

"How are you doing?" he asked, after going the entire length of the hallway. All the support she needed was for him to wrap his arm around her, but he enjoyed holding her this close and was reluctant to release her.

"Okay, that's enough for now. I'll help you get back to bed." He could see Daisy was exhausted and refused to admit it.

"I'll walk more tomorrow."

"Promise me you won't get up and try this alone."

"Okay." Even her voice was weak.

Once inside her stateroom, Asher helped Daisy back into bed and made sure she was comfortable before he left. Sometime later he went to check to be sure she hadn't overdone it. As he suspected, he found her sound asleep.

As he gazed down on her, he drew in a shaky breath. Even sick and feverish, she was lovely. He'd felt drawn to her in ways he rarely had with any woman. It'd been a long time since he'd felt this strong an attraction. Understandable, seeing that his opportunities to meet women of an appropriate age were few and far between. He'd never been great with romantic relationships and he didn't expect that to change. Locking braces with Mary Lou Chavez was the first in a short list of romances gone bad.

He had to remind himself that nothing could or should come of this attraction. In less than two weeks, Daisy would return to her busy life in Chicago, a life vastly different from his own. For his part, he'd greet the next passengers with the same enthusiasm with which he met every cruise. Life would continue as it had before, and within a month, possibly two, he would hardly remember her name.

He admired that Daisy found the gumption to go with the flow and that she enjoyed all the social and cultural opportunities available in Chicago. Having worked in remote areas for all these years, it'd been a long time since he'd taken in things like a professional baseball game or a trip to the theater, both of which he enjoyed. His brother had done his best to persuade Asher to accept a teaching position at a major university in Chicago and give up his vagabond ways, without success. Asher knew himself well enough to recognize he would never be happy living in a big city. The noise. The congestion. He'd shrivel up and die within a few months if he didn't have the space to roam in the outdoors.

He frowned, feeling sad and depressed at his thoughts, wondering at the twisted path they had taken or why he was even thinking about such matters. Almost immediately, the unwelcome answer came to him. It was Daisy.

Everly.

All he had to do was remind himself that it was Daisy he was attracted to. He suspected Everly was someone else entirely.

For a couple days Asher brought Daisy all her meals and meds. She looked forward to his visits. He often took time to chat with her, but not for nearly as long as he had earlier in her convalescence. She couldn't fault him; he was always pleasant. Something had changed, though; she wasn't sure what it was or what had happened. He seemed to be withdrawing from her in subtle ways. When she asked, he explained that he had to prepare for his lectures, although she was fairly certain they were the same ones he'd delivered a hundred times before.

It helped that she was gaining strength each day, getting out of the room and walking more. She was almost ready to join the others for meals and probably should have, except she cherished being alone with Asher.

By the end of the sixth day, she decided it was time to sit in on the lectures and join the other passengers. By then she was thoroughly sick of remaining in her stateroom. The fever was gone, and she felt almost like her old self.

Everyone aboard the Amazon Explorer had heard about her troubles. The first ones to approach her were Janice and David Brown.

"It's so good to see you up and about," Janice said, squeezing her hand as she took the seat next to Everly.

"I'm happy to be out of that stateroom, that's for sure."

"I'm so sorry you've had to miss going out on the Zodiacs," Janice continued. "We have seen the most amazing birds along the way, and the foliage is magnificent."

During his visits, Asher had often spoken with enthusiasm of the ecology system of the rainforest. Although she hadn't been the least bit interested when she first boarded the ship, he'd piqued her curiosity. After spending nearly all of her first week of the cruise in bed, she was eager to get out and explore the rainforest for herself.

She remembered Asher's comment about people being so busy in the fast pace of life that they missed out on the amazing and the spectacular that was right in front of them. Here she was in the middle of the most incredible ecosystem on earth and she fully intended to enjoy it, to open her eyes and see the things Asher spoke of with such energy and passion.

After a full seven days, all her symptoms had disappeared, and she felt like a new woman. Asher declared her healthy and fit. Everly was almost sorry that she wouldn't be seeing nearly as much of him. She spent the entire day with the other passengers, sat in on the lecture, and attended all the meals.

That evening it was announced that in a couple days the passengers would be taking the long-awaited trek into the rainforest to meet with the indigenous tribe. At dinner that night, it was all anyone would talk about.

"If you feel up to it, you really should go," Asher encouraged her after his lecture.

"I'd like that, I really would. Unfortunately, because of the mix-up, I didn't pack the appropriate gear."

Everly wasn't in her room more than fifteen minutes when there was a knock on her door.

She opened it to find Asher standing there. "As it happens, the ship has a limited gift shop with Explorer shirts and pants. Many of our passengers like to collect these as keepsakes, since the name of the ship is embroidered on the shirts. I had to guess your size. No worries if these don't fit, they can be exchanged in time for you to go on the excursion." He handed her a bag.

For half a second, Everly was speechless. "How thoughtful. Thank you, Asher."

A smile lit up his handsome face. "I would hate for you to miss it," he said. "I know once you've had the chance to explore the rainforest, you'll never be the same."

That was exactly what Everly expected would happen.

CHAPTER SIX

At six-thirty, as had happened all week, Everly was abruptly woken by a loudspeaker announcement stating that breakfast would take place in thirty minutes. She bolted upright in bed and rubbed the sleep out of her eyes. In many ways this cruise was like summer camp for adults, a reminder of a happy childhood. She stumbled out of bed and reached for the clothes Asher had delivered the night before. He must have been paying attention, because everything he'd chosen fit perfectly, as if specifically designed for her.

After breakfast, Everly and her fellow passengers gathered in the general meeting area. Asher stood before them. "This morning, I'm going to tell you about two of the most dangerous insects and spiders in the world. I imagine most of you can guess the first one."

The German professor, Gunther Kotz, raised his hand and looked sympathetically toward Everly. "The mosquito."

"Right on. Mosquitoes thrive in hot and humid environments, and the Amazon rainforest provides ideal conditions. If you didn't think to bring bug repellent with you," he said, and looked pointedly at Everly, "there is some available in the gift shop."

Everly knew she'd be making a trip there as soon as the lecture was over. Bugs, even the most benign, gave her the willies, especially after her most recent ordeal.

"Mosquitoes carry a variety of diseases, including yellow fever and malaria. So please be sure to use plenty of insect repellent anytime we are off the ship." Again, the remark seemed to be aimed at her. Everly had learned her lesson and intended to slather enough repellent on her to bring down every insect within a two-mile radius.

"And then there is the wandering spider."

Everly cringed. Spiders, by far, were one of her absolute worst fears. The thought of them sent chills down her spine.

"It is the most venomous arachnid in the world. The scientific name is the Greek word for 'murderess.'"

Everly's hand shot into the air.

"Yes, Daisy," Asher said, giving her his attention.

"How likely are we to see one of these killer spiders?"

His smile was all-knowing. "Not likely. They mostly

prowl around the jungle floor during the night, seeking out prey rather than building nests."

"Is that why they're named wandering spiders?" Professor Kotz asked.

"Makes sense," someone else called out.

"During daylight, they like to hide in various places, like in the leaves of the banana plant."

Everly gasped.

Asher sent her a reassuring glance. "The likelihood of us getting close to one is highly improbable. You can rest easy, Daisy."

"Thank you." That was encouraging, but it didn't give her a lot of confidence when it came to traipsing through the jungle, which she would be doing soon enough.

To Everly's surprise, the day flew by quickly. She had to admit the information given was enlightening and interesting. After lunch she took a short nap, found a research book in what passed for the library—she found a total of five fiction paperbacks; everything else were well-read nonfiction titles. Seeing that the only available space in her room to relax was on her bed, where she'd spent the majority of five full days, she curled up in the meeting area of the ship instead. She was soon joined by Janice Brown.

"I'm so pleased you've recovered," she said, "and even more so when Asher told us you'd be joining us tomorrow morning for the excursion."

"I'm looking forward to it. When I first came on board, I didn't have the right attitude, but hearing about the wonders of the rainforest from Asher has given me a change of heart."

What Asher had said continued to play in her mind, about having the beauty of nature directly in front of her and passing it by without noticing. Years ago, Everly had read a story about a classical musician who played at Carnegie Hall with tickets that cost as much as five hundred dollars each. He set up in the subway station and played his violin for free and collected thirty dollars. People walked right past without recognizing they were listening to a virtuoso.

"Yes, Asher's lectures have been inspiring. One can't listen to him speak and not hear his passion. It's contagious."

Asher had made the Amazon and the rainforest sound intriguing . . . much as the man was himself. He put her at ease and had seen her at her worst. She liked him, enjoyed listening to him. Not that she had any great expectations of anything lasting from their friendship. He wasn't exactly the Latin lover she'd dreamed about while on the long flight to Brazil.

In many ways he was better. Asher had awakened something inside of Everly, something that had lain dormant since she'd joined forces with Jack Campbell to create Easy Home. She was strongly attracted to Asher, drawn in by his passion and knowledge for a world that she had basically ignored once she'd moved away from the farm. He was lighting up a dark area of her life with the thought of family, friends, relationships that she had pushed aside in her drive to prove herself and make a success of the business. He made her wonder what all she'd lost out on because she'd walked through the last six years wearing blinders.

"Don't allow the reaction to that mosquito bite ruin your vacation," Janice advised. "Make the most of this opportunity. I strongly suspect you'll be able to look back at this trip as one of the highlights of your life."

"I think it just might be," she admitted. Annette had arranged this cruise as revenge; little did Jack's niece realize she'd done Everly a huge favor.

"If it will help, you can sit with me on the Zodiac," Janice suggested next. "I'm not exactly graceful when it comes to climbing in and out of those rubber rafts."

"I don't imagine I will be, either." Sitting behind a desk all day wasn't exactly conducive to leaping in and out of watercrafts. Other than when she was a kid, she wasn't much of an outdoors person. Her siblings had all been active in sports, but not Daisy. She was always the last one to be chosen for a team. Her mother insisted she had other talents, different ones. And she did.

The next morning, lathered up in mosquito repellent, dressed in her new clothes, Everly joined the others as they left the

Amazon Explorer and settled into the Zodiacs. Asher was in the same Zodiac as Everly. He seemed to be keeping an eye on her, and she was grateful, although she knew the reason. He wanted to be sure she was up to this after being sick.

Hanging on tightly, she and Janice linked their arms together in support and rode for a good twenty minutes along the murky waters of the Amazon. The Zodiac slowed as the watercraft entered a tributary. As the boat came to a near crawl, Asher pointed out several species of birds, providing names that quickly flew in and out of her head. He was knowledgeable and entertaining, adding tidbits of information. Everly found herself enjoying what he said as well as the sound of his voice, which was rich, mellow, and familiar after all the time they'd spent together.

The Zodiac entered an area where the water was still, where they happened upon lily pads as large as a child's swimming pool. The flowers were gorgeous.

"They are known as Victoria amazonica," Asher explained. "They are the world's largest lily pads and routinely grow to over ten feet in diameter and are stable enough to support the weight of a small child."

Her companions grabbed every opportunity for picture taking. Several in the Zodiac had professional cameras with a variety of lenses. She hadn't even thought to bring her phone, which she now regretted.

As if sensing her disappointment, Asher leaned toward

her and said, "I've collected a number of amazing shots over the years that I'll be happy to share with you."

"Thank you," she whispered back.

One of the women frowned, as if annoyed by the special treatment Everly got. To be fair, Everly felt a bit guilty about it as well, although she appreciated Asher's kindness and attention. It seemed Everly wasn't the only one who'd taken notice of how attractive Asher was, even if the woman was twenty years older.

With so much to see, Everly lost track of time, but it had to have been forty minutes or longer before the Zodiacs reached the spot where they were to disembark. Asher got out first and lent a hand to each one as they stepped off the rubber lip of the watercraft and onto the land.

Everly was one of the last to depart behind Janice. Asher placed his hands around her waist and half-lifted her onto dry ground so she could avoid getting her tennis shoes wet. Everyone else had boots.

"Thanks," she said, enjoying the feel of his arms as he set her down. He might have held on to her a bit longer than necessary, but maybe she was imagining that—not that she was complaining.

He held her gaze before he released her. "My pleasure." As if uncomfortable, he hurried to the front of the assembled group and led the way into the lush forest. Everly was the last passenger in the single line that snaked through the thick foliage. Jimmy, the crew member who'd manned the Zodiac, held up the rear. A light mist started to fall on them, followed by a deluge. It was as if she was standing under a waterfall, which made it nearly impossible to see. Water poured off the brim of the hat Asher had provided.

Keeping her head lowered, Everly trudged on, following Janice and stepping into her muddy footprints. She tired quickly and had trouble keeping up with the group. Jimmy was somewhere behind her. Everly paused when she came upon a fork in the path, unsure which way to go. She'd gotten confused and could no longer see Janice, who was well ahead of her. She sighed with relief when she saw footprints. She took the path and continued on, determined to catch up with the rest of the group.

After about ten minutes of walking as fast as she could in the downpour, she called out to Jimmy. "How much farther is this village?"

Her question went unanswered.

She tried again, louder this time, thinking Jimmy must not have heard her.

Again, she got no response. Lifting her head, she turned, only to realize that Jimmy wasn't there, nor could she see Janice.

She was alone and lost in the rainforest.

"Hello," she shouted, her voice shrill with panic. "Can anyone hear me?" She couldn't possibly have wandered too far away. She'd been following Janice's muddy boot prints, stepping into the same spot her friend had taken. Looking down, she realized that it wasn't a boot print she'd been blindly tracking—it was a bare footprint.

"Help," she tried again, but she could barely hear her own voice above the sound of the pounding rain. She stood under the shelter of what could well have been a banana tree until she remembered Asher's talk about the wandering spider. One could easily be hiding in the leaves. She preferred getting drenched over being bitten by a murdering spider.

Frozen, she was almost afraid to breathe. The downpour had returned to a mist, but by this point her clothes were sopping wet and clung to her.

"Why is this happening?" she cried out to the universe. If Annette had sought revenge, she'd gotten it in spades. She could see the headlines now: "Chicago Executive Lost in Amazon Rainforest."

The leaves rustled behind her and for a moment she was convinced she'd been found. Quickly she surmised that the movement might not be human but that of a wild animal. Asher had said that the jaguar made the rainforest its home. The jaguar was the third-largest big cat in the world, he'd said. He'd also mentioned they were killing machines.

"Nice kitty," she whispered.

The bush moved again. Her breathing stopped entirely as fear gripped her lungs. Never had she been more afraid in her life. She thought about her mother and siblings and re-gretted every holiday she'd missed with her family. Silently she pleaded with God that if He let her survive, she'd make it up to her family if it took her the rest of her life, which she sincerely hoped would last many years.

The brush parted. Everly's eyes widened. This was it. Ei-ther she was being rescued or she would be left for dead on the muddy floor of this jungle.

Only, it wasn't a jaguar that was behind the vegetation. It was a short man with a dark face smeared with red paint. He wore a loincloth and carried a spear.

Everly immediately relaxed. One of the Caribs, the indig-enous people they were meeting, had found her. He would take her to the others.

"Oh, thank heavens," she said, smiling at him. "I can't tell you how much I appreciate you finding me. I don't know what happened. I was right behind Janice and then I wasn't."

He stared at her and remained silent.

"It must have been your footprint that I followed. How that happened is a mystery to me. Maybe not, as there was that fork in the path. I must have chosen the wrong one. Thankfully, Asher noticed and sent you to find me."

Again, he remained silent.

"I can't imagine where Jimmy is. Have you seen him?" She was grateful when the sun broke through the canopy of trees, providing enough light for her to see.

The little man, who was no taller than five foot three, turned and indicated that she should follow him. He was amazingly agile and quickly made his way through the foliage. Everly blindly followed and did her best to keep pace.

After several minutes at this grueling pace, she badly needed to rest. Asher must have forgotten to tell him she had only recently recovered from a lengthy illness. "Would it be possible . . . for you . . . to slow down?" she asked, in a desperate effort to catch her breath. She was eager to join the others, but she wasn't sure how long she could maintain this killing pace.

The man made a grumbling sound. It amazed her how adept he was at walking through the rainforest. He might be small in stature, but he was quick and strong. Keeping up with him was difficult.

After thirty minutes, Everly found it nearly impossible to move at the same rate as her rescuer, and once more, she began to slow down. She'd assumed the village, where Asher planned to take them, would be relatively close.

How had she really gotten so far turned around?

Breathless, she stopped and planted her hands on her knees, hoping to even out her breathing. If she'd had the wherewithal, she would have explained her circumstances, but it didn't seem like the man understood a word she'd said. Every time she tried to communicate, he cocked his head to one side and gave her the strangest look.

"I need to rest," she said calmly, and pressed her hand over her heart and breathed hard, hoping he would understand.

He spoke again, and although she couldn't understand a word, he appeared to be urging her forward, indicating she should follow him.

"I'm doing the best I can," she said, and would have added more if she could catch her breath.

He paused, and then after a few moments he pointed straight ahead as if to indicate they were close to where she would meet up with the others. Only she couldn't see anything that resembled a village. That was odd. If they were close, wouldn't she hear voices?

Everly hesitated. She was beginning to have suspicions that this fellow wasn't who she thought he was. Holding up her index finger, she narrowed her gaze on him and said, "Exactly where are you taking me?"

Stepping forward, he chatted away as if she understood every word he said. He sounded perfectly reasonable, and it seemed like he wanted to help.

"I wish I understood what you're trying so hard to tell me."

Once more he pointed ahead and started walking, assuming she would follow him, and so she did.

Within a matter of minutes, they stepped into a clearing. Several other warriors milled about, all men and all with weapons. When the one who'd found her came into view a cheer rose from the other men.

This wasn't any village. This looked more like a hunting party.

"Daisy."

Hearing her name, she whirled around to find Jimmy tied to a tree.

"Jimmy?" She rushed forward, intending to untie him, and was stopped by one of the other warriors, who adamantly shook his head as if warning her.

The young man's shoulders sagged in defeat. "So sorry, Miss."

"What's happening? Why are you tied up?"

"I wish I knew. I was behind you and saw that you'd taken the wrong turn. I tried to call out and tell you that you were going the wrong way, but you couldn't hear me with the rain pounding down."

Everly felt dreadful. "Oh no, this is all my fault. Let me explain to them that you are a friend."

Turning to the group of warriors, she motioned toward Jimmy. "Friend," she said and smiled, hoping that would convey the message.

The men looked at one another and seemed uncertain. They huddled together and seemed to be making a decision of some sort. She hoped they would come to the conclusion to free Jimmy.

"This is my fault," Jimmy said. "When I couldn't see you after the fork and realized you'd taken the wrong path, I started jogging after you. Then this little fellow stepped out of the jungle, aimed his spear, and stopped me. I tried to explain, but he didn't understand. The next thing I knew I was tied to this tree."

"Do you think we're in any danger?" she asked, noting all the men were armed and now that they'd come out of their huddle were closely watching their exchange.

Jimmy snorted. "I don't know, but I have to tell you, it doesn't look good from my perspective."

Jimmy had a point.

She turned to the group of men and smiled. They all stared back at her blankly. "Would you kindly release my friend?"

They continued to stare at her as if she hadn't spoken.

"I don't think they understand English," Jimmy offered.

"Do you know any Portuguese?"

"None. What about you?" he asked hopefully.

"Oh dear," she whispered, wondering what she should try next, if anything. Why did everything have to happen to her?

A commotion arose among the men; there seemed to be a loud disagreement.

Jimmy met her gaze. "Miss, I don't think these men are from the same tribe we were planning to meet."

Everly was beginning to have the same feeling. "What do you suggest we do?"

"At this point, I don't think we have much of a choice. Remain calm and wait to be rescued."

She swallowed against the tightness in her throat. "Will Asher find us?"

Jimmy nodded, his eyes connecting with hers, offering reassurance. "He won't rest until he does."

CHAPTER SEVEN

It took longer than it should have for Asher to realize Daisy wasn't with the others. Just to be on the safe side, he counted heads a second time.

"Ms. Brown," he said calmly, despite the dread pounding in his heart, "have you seen Daisy?"

The older woman had a stricken look. "Not in a while." Suddenly aware that Daisy was missing, she glanced around their assembled group and cast him a worried frown.

"When was the last time you remember seeing her?" he asked, unable to hide his concern. Having so recently recovered from her bout with the fever, he feared she might have fallen behind and gotten lost.

She shook her head as if to help clear her mind. "I . . . I don't remember seeing her after we reached that turn . . . It looked like there might be another path heading in another direction. Until that point, I could swear she was directly behind me. I checked on her a couple times, but then it started to rain hard, and the water was pouring off the brim of my hat and I could barely see in front of me."

Seeing that his wife was upset, Mr. Brown came to stand alongside Janice. He placed a protective arm around her shoulders. "I don't recall seeing Daisy, either. At least not since we arrived here."

The native women of the small village were busy crouched down and cooking a special lunch for their visitors. This group of Caribs had been exposed to Western culture and yet had maintained their lifestyle. They had found it to be helpful to the tribe to keep their traditions when interacting with tourists such as those on the Amazon Explorer. Other groups often visited and contributed to their economy.

Asher garnered the cruise passengers' attention. "Can anyone remember seeing Daisy?" he called out.

"Where's Jimmy?" Professor Kotz asked.

In his concern about Daisy, Asher hadn't noticed that Jimmy was also missing. An immediate mixture of relief and concern knotted his stomach. While he was worried about them both, he was grateful that wherever she was, Daisy wasn't alone. Jimmy was young; this was only his third trip in Brazil and on the Amazon Explorer. All Asher could do was hope that the young man would stay with Daisy and protect her.

Alex, the Amazon Explorer's purser, approached Asher. "Stay with the group," Asher told him. "I'm going back to the river to check if that's where they might be." He silently prayed that Jimmy had sense enough to either find his way back to the river where they'd banked the Zodiac or stay put until they could be found.

"I'll go with you," Akuntsu insisted. He was the head of the tribe and was familiar with this area of the rainforest.

At first Asher was inclined to refuse, knowing the man was needed at the village, but then he quickly changed his mind. Akuntsu knew this jungle far better than Asher did. If there was a chance Daisy and Jimmy had gotten lost, the hope of finding them increased with the other man as his guide.

Moving at a clipped pace, the walk to the river took half the time it had originally. Asher's heart sank when he saw neither Daisy nor Jimmy anywhere close to the rivercraft. With nothing left to do, he reached for his walkie-talkie and radioed the ship, requesting assistance.

"We have one guest missing in the jungle," he told the captain. "I believe Jimmy might be with her. I'm searching for them now. I left Alex with the rest of the passengers."

"Let me guess which guest it is," Captain Martin muttered, clearly concerned. "It's that Daisy woman, isn't it? What did she do, decide to walk back to Chicago?"

"I don't believe so, Captain." Daisy hadn't made a good impression on Captain Martin when she'd indicated this wasn't the cruise she'd been expecting and wanted him to return to Manaus.

He heard the other man grumble under his breath. Asher filled in as many of the details as he had and requested a second Zodiac in case he didn't find Daisy and Jimmy before it was time for the other passengers to return to the ship. Captain Martin dispatched Mike, the safety officer, to join Alex and leave the second Zodiac alongside the other one.

"Come," Akuntsu said, heading into the thick jungle.

Before the excursion, Asher had mentioned the dangers that abound in the rainforest. He knew from experience how real they could be. His mind conjured up several scenarios that left his heart in a panic. Just the day before he'd spoken of the jaguar as a killing machine. If Daisy had been attacked by one it was unlikely either she or Jimmy would have survived.

Breaking away from the well-traveled path, Akuntsu squatted down to study the muddy jungle floor and veered off at the point Janice Brown had mentioned. Straightening, he examined a bush, then wordlessly started up again.

"What did you see?" Asher asked. He couldn't identify any markings that were of significance.

"Footprint."

Asher stared down at where Akuntsu pointed and couldn't make out anything other than mud.

"Come," Akuntsu called out, heading through the foliage, pausing every now and again to study the landscape or point out a plant with a bent branch.

Asher's mind raced with multiple fears. All he could do was pray that if they were together, neither had been injured.

After what felt like an eternity, Akuntsu slowed to a near crawl. When Asher asked why he'd stopped, the man raised his arm and silenced him. It took a moment before he heard voices in the distance. Frowning, Asher looked to the other man, hoping Akuntsu would be able to translate.

"Friends?" he asked in a whisper.

Akuntsu held up his hand a second time, indicating he needed silence. Minutes crawled by as they remained hidden by the jungle.

When Asher couldn't stand it any longer, he whispered another question: "What are they saying?"

Akuntsu shook his head as he strained to listen. Crouching, he crawled closer while Asher waited, growing more concerned and impatient by the minute. He didn't understand why they didn't approach the group and retrieve Daisy and Jimmy, or if they were even with this tribe.

Akuntsu returned. "No understand," he explained. "No make war?"

"War?"

"Men have weapons."

Asher couldn't even begin to imagine what Daisy had gotten herself into.

With Akuntsu in the lead, the two men approached the six men who were all well armed with both spears and dart guns angled across their torsos. As soon as the two walked into the circle, six spears were aimed in their direction. Asher stood stock-still and waited for his friend to take the lead.

Akuntsu spoke in his native tongue to the group. To Asher's relief they slowly, reluctantly lowered their weapons. One of the men pointed to Daisy and spoke quickly. Akuntsu answered and the same man adamantly shook his head.

Daisy was standing next to Jimmy, who was secured to a tree. He was grateful they were together, although he couldn't understand why the Zodiac captain was tied up. His first thought was to free him, but he figured he should wait until Akuntsu gave him the okay.

"It's all right," she said in a calm, reassuring voice, speaking to the men with spears. "These are our friends."

The warriors frowned, looking from her to Asher and then back again.

"Friend," she repeated. "Good friend." Walking over to Asher, she wound her arms around his waist and hugged him.

Automatically he welcomed her into his embrace, squeezing her hard in his relief to have found her. "Are you hurt?" he asked. Their eyes met and he drank in the sight of her, his relief so great he was afraid he might have cracked one of her ribs.

"I'm good. More than good." Smiling, she looked up at him, her eyes bright with welcome.

For the life of him, it was all Asher could do to keep from kissing her.

The warriors and Akuntsu continued their conversation, each speaking rapidly in a language Asher had no hope of understanding. With his arms still around Daisy's waist, holding her close to his side, he turned his attention to his guide. "What are they saying?" Asher needed an explanation.

"Words not same," Akuntsu said, cutting off his conversation with the other man. "If I understand . . . they think they save woman from evil."

"Evil?" Asher repeated.

One of the warriors pointed at Jimmy.

"Jimmy," Asher asked. "Do you know what they mean?"

The same warrior spoke again and Akuntsu nodded. "He say . . . woman go wrong way. Man run after her. He stop man. Save woman."

"You thought I was in danger?" Daisy asked, her voice low and melodious. Breaking away from Asher, she approached one of the warriors. "Thank you." She held out her hand for him to shake, but he stared at her with a horrified expression. After an awkward moment she withdrew her hand. "That is so wonderful of you, but I was in no real danger . . . well, other than from a wandering spider and maybe a jaguar."

As though alarmed, the warrior leaped back and spoke quickly to Akuntsu, adamantly shaking his head.

Akuntsu shook his head. "No. No."

"What's happening?" Asher asked.

Akuntsu turned away so that his back was to the small group of men. "When woman offer hand, he think she want him for husband. He say you can have her. He has one wife and she is all he can feed."

"He thought what?" Daisy asked, looking stunned.

Asher stifled a laugh. "Tell him I thank him and claim her."

"What?" Daisy whirled around.

"Hey," Jimmy called out irritably. "In case anyone's noticed, I'm still tied up here."

"You didn't really mean it when you said you'd claim me, did you?"

Her eyes met his, and for the life of him Asher couldn't look away.

"Hey, guys," Jimmy called, louder this time, distracting him. "Remember me?"

As if hearing Jimmy for the first time, Asher untied Jimmy, who, once free, rubbed the feeling back into his wrists and scowled at Daisy. "I hate to break up this romantic reunion, but I'd appreciate it if we could get back to the ship."

Asher thanked Akuntsu and the warriors for looking

after Daisy. Akuntsu led them out of the jungle. Unwilling to risk losing her again, Asher reached for Daisy's hand, intent on keeping her close.

Her hand curved around his, holding on tightly. "Jimmy said you'd come," Daisy said, staying close by his side.

"I wasn't going to lose you . . . or Jimmy," he added, almost as an afterthought.

"Thank you . . . I had no idea what was happening or why. They were all wonderful, don't you think? I can't wait to tell my family about this. They won't believe this adventure . . . and to think that sweet little man assumed I wanted him as my husband. This is a story I'll tell my grandchildren one day." She sounded almost giddy.

That evening, as the exploration group gathered for the social hour before dinner, Asher was asked to explain the events of that morning and afternoon. Now that Daisy and Jimmy were safe, their story circulated among the passengers faster than an online virus.

"As you recall, I mentioned a while back that there were as many as seventy-seven uncontacted indigenous groups in Brazil. Well, thanks to Daisy and Jimmy, there are now only seventy-six."

A small rumble of laughter filled the room.

"Daisy and our Jimmy were taken by six warriors. We

owe a debt of gratitude to Akuntsu, whom many of you met earlier. The warriors from a different tribe were on a hunting expedition when they came upon our group and thought to rescue Daisy."

"Were they going to eat Daisy and Jimmy?" one of the women asked.

Asher assumed the question was a joke and soon realized it wasn't. While tempted to smile, he held back his amusement. "I don't believe that was their intent."

Keeping an eye on Daisy, he noticed that her face was red with embarrassment at being the focus of attention. She repeatedly apologized to everyone involved in her rescue, despite the number of assurances Asher gave her that none of what happened was her fault.

Looking to turn the conversation away from the events of the afternoon, Asher motioned toward the piano. "The holiday season is upon us. I thought it might be a bit of fun if we gathered around and sang a few carols before heading into dinner. Does anyone here play?"

The room went silent for several seconds before Daisy raised her hand. "It's been a while, but I used to play quite a bit."

"Thank you, Daisy. We'd appreciate it if you'd lead us in a few classic Christmas carols."

She moved to the piano and sat down on the bench. Sighing, she placed her hands reverently over the keys and waited, as if searching her memory for the notes. After a short pause she expertly ran through the introduction to three of the most familiar holiday songs before settling into "Jingle Bells." It was an upbeat, familiar song. When it seemed everyone was enraptured by her expert playing, Asher started the singing, and soon Daisy's sweet voice blended in with his. It wasn't long before several others joined in. When it came to "O Christmas Tree," the professor and his wife sang beautifully in their native tongue. Their performance was followed by loud applause and appreciation.

Asher sat down on the piano bench next to Daisy and led the singing from one song to the next. When the dinner bell rang, he offered her his hand.

"That was great. Thank you."

"Thank you," she said, and elbowed him in the ribs. "I know what you were doing. That was a clever way to cut short the inquisition about Jimmy and my grand adventure."

As they joined the line for dinner, Asher was called away by Captain Martin. When he returned to the dining room, he noticed that Daisy's table was full. He sat with Professor Kotz and his wife and enjoyed a lively dinner conversation.

Asher seldom had trouble sleeping. Being on the river relaxed him and it was rare for it to take more than a few minutes for him to drift into slumber. This night, however, his mind raced with the speed of a high-powered car in the Indy 500. He couldn't stop thinking about how good it had felt to hold Daisy. He'd been half out of his mind with the thought of her lost in the jungle. Yet when he found her, she was cool and calm, thinking it was the experience of a lifetime. Yes, she was embarrassed that she had inconvenienced others; he could appreciate her concern, but like he'd reminded her, none of what happened was her fault.

While she'd been ill, he'd enjoyed spending time with her, going above and beyond anything he would normally have done for another under-the-weather passenger. She made him forget his awkwardness and put him at ease. Somewhere along the way he grew comfortable with her and free to share his life and a few stories of where the Explorer cruises had taken him around the world. She seemed genuinely interested and asked him question after question until he forgot to be nervous. He enjoyed their three-questions game, and had learned a lot about her life, too, her drive and ambition, the fact that she felt like the odd man out with her family. It seemed natural to talk and laugh with her. Repeatedly he had to remind himself that in another few days, she would disembark and return to her life. Nothing was going to happen in the time they had left. Once she was gone, nothing would change and life would go on as before.

After an hour of tossing and turning, seeking out a comfortable position, Asher decided to get up. He quickly dressed and decided he'd seek out a book in the library area, which was in an alcove off the main meeting room. Most of the nonfiction ones he'd read several times over. The fiction paperbacks were those left behind by guests. Asher was in the mood for a story, thinking reading might help put him to sleep.

As he entered the small alcove, he noticed someone else was sitting on the bench there. His heart sped up when he realized it was Daisy.

She looked up when she noticed he'd joined her. She sat on the bench with her long legs tucked to one side and had a blanket wrapped around her.

"You couldn't sleep, either?" he asked, sitting down next to her.

"No. My head was spinning, thinking about today. I had such a lovely time, despite everything. Is that what's keeping you awake?"

"I hadn't given it much thought. Possibly. I normally don't have trouble sleeping. I find being on the water soothing."

"I do, too, although tonight is the exception."

Sitting down next to her, he reached for her hand. His heart seemed to be jumping up and down in his chest like it was on a trampoline. He was sure his face was heated. He was grateful the alcove was in the shadows.

Her fingers tightened around his. "Thank you, Asher, for finding us."

"All part of the service offered aboard the Amazon Explorer." No way would he have gone back to the boat and left her and Jimmy behind.

The tension between them grew thick, and, unsure what it meant or what he should do, he asked, "Why are you out here instead of in your room?"

"After spending an entire week in my stateroom, I thought I'd come here."

"I'm glad you did."

"I'm glad you're here."

He smiled at her.

"You mentioned the first night of the cruise that your brother lives in Chicago. Do you ever visit?" she asked with a hopeful lilt.

He looked down at their joined hands. "On occasion. Like I mentioned earlier, I'm uncomfortable in the city."

"Oh."

"I have a contract with the Amazon Explorer that pretty much ties me up. It's hard for me to get away for any length of time."

"I see."

Her disappointment was hard to miss; he felt he should explain. "By the time I fly back to the States, it's almost time to return."

"That makes sense."

He hoped that was regret he heard in her voice. Already

his mind was looking for ways to make an exception, find a way. He quickly dismissed the thought. When Daisy left the cruise, that was it. The end. No need to involve his heart, because in the end there was no way they would be able to blend their two worlds.

"My brother's been after me for a while to visit, but he's always busy. I did mention that he's a heart surgeon, didn't I?"

"You did. If I ever experience heart troubles I'll know where to go," she said.

At the moment, Asher felt in desperate need of a heart specialist. "Daisy," he said, his voice low and full of emotion. "Today."

"Yes?"

"I . . . I couldn't bear not knowing what had happened to you."

"Well, yes," she said, making light of his comment. "Losing a passenger wouldn't look good on your job résumé."

He frowned. "It's more than keeping my job. With you, it's personal." Unable to resist her a moment longer, he gathered her in his arms and kissed her. He could tell she was surprised at first, because she tensed before she relaxed. Her arms went around his neck and she scooted up to her knees and leaned in to him. He ravaged her mouth, unable to get enough of her, taste enough of her. How long they kissed he didn't know. When they drew apart, Daisy pressed her forehead to his and released a deep sigh. He closed his eyes and continued to hold her. This woman. He didn't know what it was about her, but she drew him in unlike anyone he'd ever known.

CHAPTER EIGHT

Everly barely slept. Asher had kissed her, and it had been wonderful. Better than wonderful. It'd been years since she'd felt anything close to what she had when Asher pulled her into his arms. She felt giddy just thinking about it.

Her entire life she'd hated her name. It made her sound like her family had picked her up at a plant nursery. Several times between kisses Asher had softly whispered her name. Even though she'd told him she went by Everly, he continued to call her Daisy. He'd made it sound like one of the most beautiful words in the English language. When he said it in that special way she could almost get to like her given name.

Staring up at the ceiling in her tiny stateroom, Everly closed her eyes and let the memory of the closeness she'd felt toward him wash over her. Now that it was morning, she could barely wait to see him again, barely wait to tell him how much his kisses had meant to her.

By the time the captain's voice came over the loudspeaker system, announcing it was time to rise for breakfast, Everly was up, dressed, and ever-so-eager to see Asher. She needed to know if he felt the same way she did. They'd sat and talked for hours, then kissed and talked some more.

To her disappointment, Asher wasn't at breakfast. Break-fast and lunch were served buffet-style. Once she had filled her plate with scrambled eggs, bacon, and an English muffin, she took her seat at an empty table, hoping if Asher did arrive that he would choose to join her.

Janice Brown came to sit with her and was followed by her husband. "We so enjoyed the piano playing last night. You said it had been some time since you'd played, but it didn't show," the older woman said after taking a seat and neatly spreading her paper napkin across her lap.

"Yes . . . I didn't realize how much I've missed it. I don't have a piano in my condo. I played quite a bit growing up. Our family is musical. All my siblings play one instrument or another."

"That's wonderful."

Janice's comments reminded Everly of the fun she'd had with her musically talented family over the years. It was where she fit in most. She might not be able to compete on a soccer field, but she could race her fingers up and down a keyboard with the best of them. One tradition she'd enjoyed was the Christmas Eve hayride the entire family took through town, singing beloved carols to shut-ins and first responders, along with family and friends. The previous Christmas she'd chosen work over spending time with her siblings. A decision she regretted.

"It's good to see that you've recovered from your adventures from yesterday," David said.

Everly brightened and sat up straighter. "It was amazing to meet those warriors and get a glimpse of their culture. I believe getting lost in the rainforest might possibly be the highlight of my Amazon adventure."

"We were all quite worried about you," Janice said, as she delicately spread strawberry jam across her toast.

"None more than Asher," her husband added. "He's quite levelheaded normally, but that went out the window when he realized you were missing."

Everly felt a chill of excitement race down her spine. Surely Asher would be concerned about any passenger who appeared to be lost in the rainforest, but she couldn't help but feel that with her it was personal.

"That's not normally how he responds, and we should know," Janice added.

"How do you mean?"

David answered. "Five years ago, Janice and I were on an

Antarctica cruise and Asher was the naturalist aboard the ship. It was the experience of a lifetime."

Nodding, Janice agreed. "David and I signed up with only a handful of others to go kayaking."

"In Antarctica?" Everly was shocked.

"Yes," Janice said, smiling proudly. "It was the most exciting thing I've ever done. David talked me into it, and I was glad he did, especially when I consider what happened."

"I can't even imagine doing such a thing," Everly said, and she meant it. Give her a cozy spot in front of the fireplace with a good book and she was happy.

"Oh, it was quite the adventure. The worst part for me was transfering from the Zodiac into the kayak and then from the kayak back into the Zodiac," Janice said.

"You're getting us sidetracked, honey," David said, cutting her off.

"Sorry, dear. I tend to do that."

David gently patted her hand.

"What I wanted to tell you was that Asher was the head of our group and while we were in the water a pod of whales surrounded us. I don't remember being more frightened in my life," Janice said, trembling slightly with the memory.

"I don't think there was one of us who wasn't terrified of what could happen."

Janice placed her hand over her heart. "My biggest fear was getting tossed out of the kayak and into the frigid waters . . . Of course, we had on protective watertight gear . . . Still, the possibility left me terrified. Only heaven knows what those huge whales would have done once we were flapping around in the icy waters. They might have viewed us as their next meal."

"It must have been horrifying," Everly said. It certainly wasn't a situation she'd ever want to experience.

"Like I said, Asher was with us and handled the situation beautifully," David said.

"He was wonderful," Janice agreed with a nod.

"He calmly had us form a circle together and told us to remain stationary with our oars out of the water. He spoke to us, soothing our fears, and said we should enjoy this rare opportunity of viewing whales in the wild."

"Once we relaxed and the orcas swam up close to our circle, we were able to observe these marvelous creatures in a way few will ever have the opportunity to experience."

"It was magnificent," Janice said.

"It was the highlight of our trip," David concurred.

Janice smiled. "Christmas card–worthy. The best part was that David was able to get photos!"

"My point is," David continued, "Asher was completely calm through that entire episode. Yet when he discovered you were missing yesterday, he was beside himself with worry, barking orders, asking questions. It left us all shaken because we know he generally is a rock in these types of situations."

Everly smiled, hoping to hide how pleased his reaction made her feel. He did care about her above how he would for another passenger. When he'd held and kissed her, he'd repeatedly mentioned how alarmed he'd been when he realized she was lost. Remembering his words warmed her romantic heart, the very heart that had lain dormant for far too long.

"I believe Asher is quite taken with you," Janice said, lowering her voice to a whisper. "And I, for one, think it's delightful. You're both young and unattached. While we don't know you well, we've had the opportunity to spend time with Asher twice now and we both think he's a wonderful young man."

Everly blushed like a schoolgirl. She was out of her element; if Jack or anyone in the office at Easy Home could see her now, they wouldn't believe she was the same woman. To hide her pleasure, she paid close attention to her breakfast.

"Janice," David warned, "you're making Daisy uncomfortable. We need to change the subject."

"I apologize, Daisy."

"Nonsense," Everly said. The two had made her morning.

In an obvious change of subject, Janice asked, "What are your plans for this Christmas? It'll be here before you know it."

"I'm heading to Indiana to be with family." She regretted being away from them the last couple years.

"That's great."

"It's a little hectic. All my siblings are married with children. It's a madhouse for sure, but my parents wouldn't have it any other way."

"You're sure to have a marvelous time."

"What about the two of you?" Everly asked, certain the couple was like her own family-orientated parents.

"Our son and daughter and our five grandchildren will be joining us. We were on a cruise last Christmas and I don't think they'll ever forgive us."

"We promised not to do that again," David said, chuckling softly. "You'd think we'd disinherited the children from the way they acted."

"Was it another Explorer expedition?" The Browns seemed to enjoy these cruises, and like nearly everyone else, this wasn't their first adventure with the company.

"Not this time; we went the luxury route on one of those fancy cruise ships from Singapore to Hong Kong, and it was splendid. I'd do it again, just not over Christmas."

The purser's voice came over the speaker and announced that Asher would be giving another lecture and asked for everyone to gather in the meeting area in fifteen minutes.

Asher knew he should never have kissed Daisy. He'd lowered his guard and did the very thing he swore he wouldn't do:

become emotionally involved with Daisy. If he was looking for an excuse, he'd blame his lack of discipline on the stress of that afternoon, when he discovered her missing. When he'd gone down for the night, his mind refused to rest. All he could think about was Daisy and the relief he felt when she'd been found. He hadn't even realized Jimmy was missing until someone pointed it out. All he could focus on was Daisy.

His mistake was venturing into the meeting area. Or more specifically, not going back to his room when he found Daisy there. He'd had no idea she would be curled up reading there. It had been a weak moment, the two of them alone, moonlight spilling over her. He couldn't imagine any woman more beautiful than Daisy in that instant. He knew he was going to kiss her, knew he wouldn't be able to stop himself, and so he'd given in to the impulse and woke with a hundred regrets.

Nothing would come of this short fling. In another five days she would be out of his life and he would be out of hers. The attraction they felt toward each other was situational and would quickly fade. If he wasn't careful, things could easily get out of hand, and that was something Asher fully intended to avoid.

Unsure how best to deal with what he'd started, he spent a good portion of what remained of the night arguing with himself. By morning, he decided his only option was to put as much distance between himself and Daisy as the cruise allowed.

No more surreptitious glances. No more seeking her out at mealtimes. No more lengthy chats. And definitely no more kissing. It wouldn't be easy. Even in this short amount of time, he'd grown accustomed to her company and enjoyed it more than he wanted to admit. He needed to start now. Today.

Coward that he was, he skipped breakfast, fearing Daisy would be too much of a temptation. He spent the time he was normally at breakfast building up his resolve to avoid her as much as possible while still maintaining a friendly camaraderie. When the time arrived to give his lecture, he was ready to face Daisy.

Everly sat in the first row, front and center, for the lecture, eager to see Asher. For his previous lectures, she'd sat in the middle. Choosing a position in the front row was sure to relay the message that she was eager to see him.

The room filled up quickly with the other passengers before he appeared. Her wish was that when he saw her, he'd acknowledge her with a smile and talk to her before he started his lecture.

He didn't. In fact, he acted as if she was invisible.

"Good morning," he said, smiling and looking out over the group. He seemed to have a warm welcome for everyone but her.

Unable to hide her disappointment, Everly looked down at her hands. The woman sitting in the chair next to her brought out her knitting. Everly wished she'd had something to occupy herself, as she felt like she was naked. She needed something that would take her mind off the way Asher had ignored her.

"This morning I'd like to talk to you about the animals you can expect to see this afternoon as we slowly traverse the river."

"Dangerous ones?"

Everly welcomed the question. True, she had an irrational fear of spiders, but that wasn't all. Snakes were by far her biggest fear. Her brothers had taken delight in chasing her with garden snakes. Every time she ran across one, she'd scream like the barn had caught fire. Her father would come running and Jeff and John would dissolve into laughter. She could only imagine the dangerous snakes that populated the Amazon.

"There's always danger in the Amazon, although not all animals are to be feared. For example, the capybara."

A photo of the rodent was shown on the screen.

"The capybara is the largest rodent in the world," Asher explained. "They can weigh as much as one hundred forty pounds. They enjoy the water, so it won't be difficult for us to spot one or even several. They live in groups of ten to thirty, and it isn't uncommon to see larger groupings. On the last cruise we came upon a hundred of them."

"I've never heard of the capybara," one of the other passengers said.

"I wouldn't expect you had unless you've spent time in South America. They are fascinating creatures. And while you're looking for the capybara you might be lucky enough to see the Amazon River pink dolphin."

"There are dolphins in the Amazon?"

"Did you say pink?" someone else asked.

"Yes, pink, but they don't resemble their more familiar cousins. They have a rather long snout that looks something like a beak and a rounded head. Unfortunately, they have been threatened in recent years by pollution. Many of the local tribes view them as magical creatures."

"Do you think we'll have the chance to see one?"

"If we're fortunate," Asher said.

The talk was interesting and informative, as all of Asher's lectures had been. Listening to him, she couldn't help hearing the passion in his voice as he spoke about nature. She could tell how eager he was to share his love of all things having to do with nature.

Asher did more than lecture about the wildlife they might encounter; his talks included his feelings and his opinions when it came to preserving, restoring, and maintaining natural habitats. Being that she wasn't much of an outdoors person, especially in recent years, Everly hadn't given much thought to the environment other than on Earth Day. She recycled her garbage and brought her own grocery shopping bags on the rare occasion she went into a supermarket. However, when it came to preserving the natural environment, especially those areas designated as wilderness, she was completely ignorant.

In the question-and-answer time, one of the men asked, "What's the most dangerous fish in the Amazon River?"

Asher grinned. "Funny you should ask. It's the red-bellied piranha, which you might be surprised to learn is good eating."

"People eat piranha?"

"They do, and if luck is with us, we'll have an opportunity ourselves to enjoy a taste in the next day or two."

A murmur rose from the crowd. "How's that?"

Again, Asher was all smiles. "We'll be taking the Zodiacs out on a fishing expedition."

"For piranha?"

"Or whatever else we can hook, although the area where I'll be taking you is mostly known for the piranha."

"What about snakes?" asked an older gray-haired woman. "I'm not going if there's a chance we might see any snakes. I'm deathly afraid of them."

Everly was happy someone else brought up the question of snakes.

"Rest assured," Asher said, "most of the snakes that inhabit the rainforest are nonvenomous. Naturally, there are a few we would want to avoid. The pit viper being one of the most dangerous. And of course there's the boa constrictor and the bushmaster, the South American rattlesnake, and the green anaconda."

"Enough." The same woman who'd asked the question held up her hand. "I've heard more than I care to know."

Everly agreed. If she was going to die, she didn't want it to be from a snakebite. The mosquito was bad enough.

They took a short break for coffee and snacks before Larry, the professional photographer, gave his presentation. Seeing how Asher had ignored her all morning, she didn't seek him out. He'd made it clear that he wasn't interested in talking to her. Several of the group surrounded him with questions they hadn't had a chance to ask during the lecture.

Everly hung back, holding a cup of coffee in her hand. When it was time for Larry to give his presentation, Asher left the meeting area and walked directly past Everly without acknowledging her.

A sick feeling settled in the pit of her stomach. She supposed this was his way of saying he regretted kissing her. A numb feeling settled over her. This was why she didn't get involved in relationships. She didn't know what she could have possibly done that had changed in a matter of hours. One thing he needed to know was that she wasn't into playing these sorts of games. If he wanted to avoid her, then so be it. She was a big girl and could accept his decision with grace.

Larry gave his presentation, and even with effort, Everly doubted that she heard a single word. The screen was filled with a variety of pictures. From the sounds of appreciation coming from the audience, they must have been breathtaking. Everly barely noticed.

Following the two lectures was lunch. Everly got in line with the others and chose an empty table after she got her food. A couple she hadn't spoken with before joined her. It shouldn't have surprised her that they were full of questions about her adventures from the day before. She assured them it had been a rather exciting experience once she learned the warriors were looking out for her best interest.

With her back to the entrance, she sensed immediately when Asher entered the dining room. He collected his plate and came into view. He glanced around the room and seemed to briefly notice that there was an empty space at her table before pointedly moving on and taking a seat elsewhere.

Everly felt her heart trip over the slight and made a determined effort to smile and pretend she hadn't noticed. She finished her lunch and enjoyed her conversation with the couple, who delighted in reliving their adventures from their trip to Egypt. Their enthusiasm was contagious and Everly asked several questions, determined to make the trip one day herself.

The afternoon sped by quickly. The Zodiacs were lowered for a river ride, as they were most days. She purposely chose to board the one without Asher. No need to make it uncomfortable for them both. Alex did an excellent job of pointing out the highlights along the waterway, and the beauty and her fascination with what she saw thankfully distracted her a bit. Everly would always remember when they happened upon a family of capybaras. She was amazed at how large the rodents were, and delighted in watching them interact with one another.

When they returned, she washed her face and hands before joining everyone for the social hour before dinner. Asher was decidedly absent, and when Alex asked if she'd mind playing the piano again, she readily agreed, providing musical entertainment before they went in for dinner. A Christmas tree had been set up and there were boughs strung up along the windows. A wreath had been added to the door of her stateroom. Christmas was definitely in the air.

At the meal she sat with Professor Kotz and his wife, Miriam. The two were quite the world travelers. She enjoyed learning about their trips to all seven continents. This was their fourth trip to South America. Hearing about all there was to see and do in the world, both from the Kotzes and the couple from lunch, whet her appetite to explore and learn from different cultures herself.

Asher did make a showing for dinner. It came as no surprise that he sat elsewhere. After the meal, tired from the day's activities, Everly returned to her stateroom, determined to remain alone for the rest of the evening.

She read for an hour, and by nine-thirty she yawned and

decided to make it an early night and readied for bed. As she walked toward her tiny bathroom, she noticed that someone had slipped an envelope under her door. For a long minute all she did was stare at it. Finally overcome by curiosity, she reached down and grabbed hold of it. Inside, in slanting cursive handwriting that could belong only to Asher, he'd written:

Meet me at midnight in the alcove.

CHAPTER NINE

One character trait in Everly's life that was in abundant supply was pride. After the way Asher had blatantly ignored her all day, now out of the blue he wanted a clandestine meeting? Not happening. As far as she was concerned, he could sit in the dark and wait all by his lonesome self. Since he'd seen fit to pretend she didn't exist, she would do the same when it came to him. That seemed fair to her.

Her decision made, she threw back the covers and climbed into bed. Ideally, she would instantly fall asleep and wake refreshed in the morning. By all rights, that's exactly what should have happened, especially since she'd been nearly sleepless the night before. Instead, she found herself glancing at the clock every fifteen minutes and cursing under her breath, angry when she found it impossible to sleep. She squeezed her eyes shut, determined to push Asher Adams out of her mind. Of course, exactly the opposite happened. To her dismay, he was all she could think about.

Midnight came and went. At twelve-fifteen she heard a soft knock against her door. "Daisy."

Uncertain if she was hearing things, she rolled over so she faced the door.

Another knock, a bit louder this time. "Daisy."

Sitting up in bed, Everly crossed her arms. Asher could pound the door down if he liked; no way was she going to open it for him.

An entire minute passed, and she heard a thud against her door as if he'd braced his head there. "Please, Daisy."

His plea made her weak. Her shoulders slumped and she grudgingly tossed aside the covers and walked across the room. He stood on one side of the door and she was on the other. "What do you want?" she whispered, wondering if he could hear her.

"To talk to you."

"Just leave, Asher." She wasn't up to this game he seemed to want to play.

"I can't."

"Yes, you can. All you have to do is turn around and walk away."

"Let me explain," he pleaded.

"No explanation needed. I got your message."

"Give me five minutes. That's all I ask."

As tempting as it was to turn him down, the urgency in his voice held her transfixed. Her shoulders sagged as she sighed. "Oh, all right," she grumbled ungraciously. "Let me get dressed and I'll meet you in the alcove."

"Thank you." His words were heavy with relief.

She listened as he walked away. Taking her own sweet time, she pulled on pants and a light sweater, and then slowly made her way to where she knew Asher would be waiting. When she arrived, she saw him pacing. He must have heard her soft footsteps because he turned and started toward her.

She stretched out her arm, stopping him from getting any closer. "You have five minutes, and you're down to four and a half, so I suggest you say whatever it is you have to say and be done with it. I'm tired and I want to go back to bed."

"I wanted to apologize."

The reason he sought her out was because he felt guilty. "Apology accepted." She started to leave.

"I have four minutes left," he reminded her.

"Asher, listen, you don't need to say anything more. I get it; it's fine. I'm a big girl. One thing you should know about me is that I don't play games. You regret what happened between us last night. I understand. Don't worry. It wasn't anything more than a few kisses."

"But that's it, Daisy. I don't regret it."

He certainly had her fooled. She crossed her arms and

resisted tapping her foot, growing impatient. From the way he fidgeted, she could tell he was struggling to find the right words. Looking confused, he stabbed his hands through his hair. She resisted reminding him time was ticking away.

"I don't regret kissing you," he said again. "For the rest of the night, you were all I could think about. This happiness, this sense of wonder, kept bubbling up inside of me, but then it hit me." He paused pacing long enough to hold her gaze for several pulsating seconds.

"What hit you?" she asked.

He gestured toward her. "Don't you see? We might as well live in different worlds. Nothing is ever going to come of this. I know it and you must, too. I'm strongly attracted to you; I have been since the first day you arrived and announced you'd die without access to the Internet.

"After we kissed and I had time to think, I realized if I let it happen, I could lose my very heart to you. I know I'm putting too much credence on a few kisses, but there's something you need to understand . . ." He hesitated, as if he wasn't sure he should continue.

"Go on," she said, needing to know.

He ran his hand over his face before he spoke. "You might think I'm the kind of man who floats easily from one relationship to another. You know, a girl in every port, that sort of thing. Well, I'm not like that. I've had a couple relationships over the years, and when they ended, I was devastated.

It took months to feel like myself again. I want to avoid that kind of pain, and I could see that happening with you."

Her resolve to maintain an emotional distance was melting faster than ice cream in a Chicago heat wave.

"I know what you mean." Everly had a few of her own relationships that had gone south. They'd left her huddled in bed in a fetal position with the covers over her head, wrapped up in self-pity. If there was one thing she hated, it was crying, and she cried ugly. Her first lost love had been in college, and Lance had broken if off with her after he'd graduated, dumping her while she still had another year of school left as he went about his merry way. Then there was Dave. They'd been together almost a year, and Everly was beginning to think he might be the one. He broke it off, claiming she was married to her job. In retrospect, he wasn't all that wrong.

"It would be way too easy to give you my heart, Daisy."

That didn't sound so bad to her. She'd been attracted to Asher from the first day of the cruise as well. He had been the best of caregivers while she'd been sick. They'd spent countless hours together, getting to know each other, laughing once she was better. It had been intimate and special in ways unlike any other relationship she'd had.

Lowering her gaze, she soaked in his words. "I'm not sure what you're saying in light of today."

"Don't you understand?"

"Apparently not. Explain it to me."

"If we continued the way we were headed, knowing myself, when the time came, I was going to have a difficult time letting you go. I'd be miserable, missing you, wondering if there was a way for us to make something of this. And I have to accept that there isn't."

"In other words, quit before you start? Sounds rather pessimistic to me."

"Be reasonable, Daisy. More than once you've told me how much energy you get from living in Chicago. You've talked endlessly about all the things you love about being part of the city. Your company means the world to you. You've dedicated everything to making it a success. That's the way I feel about what I do. Sharing my passion for nature is what excites me most."

He had a valid point.

"So explaining all this is why you wanted to see me tonight?" She had to admit he looked utterly miserable.

"I thought if I ignored you it'd be easier for us to part. It didn't work. It didn't come close to working. I've felt wretched all day and I knew I couldn't continue this charade. It was much harder than I imagined, and I realized I'd gone about this all wrong. You deserved to know my reasoning."

He held her gaze, waiting for she knew not what. Everly took a step in his direction. "Thank you for explaining."

He nodded. "It's not working, Daisy. Try as I might, I can't make myself ignore you."

"Do you feel better for clearing the air?" she asked.

"I don't know," he said. "I'm having an extremely difficult time not kissing you again."

She edged a bit closer. "If you were to kiss me, you should know I wouldn't object."

Asher's face broke into a huge grim. He slipped his arms around her, embracing her as if she was the rip cord that would open his parachute. A deep, lengthy sigh moved through him as if this was the first deep breath he'd taken that day.

When they broke apart, Everly looked into his beautiful eyes. "Where do we go from here?" she asked in a husky whisper.

Asher pressed his forehead against hers. "Heaven help me, I don't have a clue."

Everly didn't, either. They sat together, Asher's arm around her as she leaned against him, her head on his shoulder.

"Three questions?" he asked, kissing the side of her face.

"How about you tell me three things I don't know about you?" she suggested.

"Okay." She sensed his smile. "One. My brother is ten years older than I and we've always been close."

"Ten years?" For whatever reason, she'd assumed they were closer in age.

"I believe I was something of a surprise to my parents," he said.

"A very good one, no doubt."

He chuckled. "That I don't know. Here's something else you don't know about me. I read a lot of science fiction. Alien worlds excite me. I've been known to stay up all night reading, unable to put the book down."

"How genre-oriented of you! And you had the nerve to tease me about my romance novels."

"And three. I got a blue ribbon at the county fair for the pet rabbit I raised. I named her Honey Bunny."

Everly laughed. "You're not much for originality, are you?"

"I have no defense. Honey Bunny was the sweetest rabbit, all white and fluffy."

She grinned. "I think you must have a romantic heart yourself but are unwilling to admit it."

Asher wiggled his eyebrows, teasing her. "Okay, your turn. Three things that I don't know about you."

She paused to think; she'd told him so much about herself already. "I won the school spelling bee when I was in the fourth grade."

"Over the entire school?"

"Yup." It had been a proud moment.

"You were always at the top of your class, weren't you?"

She nodded without bragging or elaborating how she'd graduated at the top of her class and magna cum laude from college.

"You should know I'm a creative speller," Asher admitted.

She could feel his smile against the side of her face.

Everly cocked her head to look at him. "I have a good head for business, but I love to bake bread."

"Nice."

"The problem is I also enjoy eating it, so I resist and bake only once a month."

"Such restraint is admirable. Okay, your last confession for the evening."

Everly smiled. She'd never admitted this to anyone. "I read Lily's journal that she hid under her mattress. It was scandalous."

Asher chuckled. "Did she ever find out?"

"I wouldn't be alive if she had."

"Can I ask you a question?"

"Of course." Although she wondered what it might be.

"You say you prefer to be called Everly. Is that a family name?"

"No, it's the name I chose for myself."

"Why?"

"Come on, Asher. Do you honestly think anyone would take me seriously as a businesswoman with the name Daisy?"

He nodded, but she could see that he was frowning.

"You'll always be Daisy to me," he said, and kissed her again.

The following morning, Everly and several of the others boarded the Zodiacs to head out for piranha fishing. Asher made sure Everly was in his watercraft. When she boarded, his gaze met hers and he smiled. He held on to her hand longer than necessary and winked at her when she got settled with the others. She shared the boat with David and Janice Brown and the Kotz couple. They were all equipped with fishing gear.

"Here's to another grand adventure," David said, smiling over at his wife and Everly.

Janice scooted closer to Everly and patted her hand. "What did I tell you?" she said under her breath. "That young man is crazy about you."

Everly smiled and caught Asher staring at her. She was convinced he'd heard Janice Brown and was doing his best to pretend otherwise.

"It's hard to think that in a few days we'll all be heading back to celebrate the holidays. Being here in the Amazon feels unreal. All too soon it'll be over."

That was exactly what Asher had said. She'd done a lot of thinking after their conversation. Sleep hadn't come until the wee hours of the morning. He had a point about them living in different worlds. But then she remembered how good it had felt in his arms and how his kisses had made her feel.

When the time came, and it was fast approaching, she would need to walk away, and he would need to let her go.

When she returned to the city, Everly was determined to make a change in her life. She'd taken on far more responsibility than one person could or should handle. Jack had no idea what he'd done when he insisted she take the entire month of December off. Everly was convinced he would live to regret that decision.

The longer Everly was out of the office, the more she realized how stressed out she was and how badly she needed to slow down and have a life. This vacation had opened her eyes to how she'd fallen victim to her own need to succeed. She'd given up Christmas with her family, lost out on relationships, worked tirelessly—and for what?

The engine on the Zodiac roared as it plowed forward, nearly unseating her. The action abruptly pulled her out of her thoughts.

"I never thought in a million years that I'd go piranha fishing," Janice said. "David takes me places I'd never thought of or imagined."

Everly couldn't wait to tell her dad and brothers about some of what she'd seen and done. As ardent fishermen themselves, they would be impressed when they learned she'd hooked a piranha, which she was determined to do.

The Zodiac came to a stop. "This is an area rich with aquatic life."

"Lots of piranha, you say?"

Asher nodded. "The best spot I've found. With luck, everyone will catch one or more fish. Remember, this is our dinner," he teased. "You don't catch a piranha, then you go hungry,"

"Don't you worry, sweetheart," David said to Janice. "I'll catch your share as well."

"I'll catch my own, thank you," she returned, and grabbed hold of her fishing pole.

"As will I," Everly announced. "I'm a farm girl, with some experience fishing." She didn't mention that her dad had to bait her line because the thought of touching a slimy worm disgusted her and her sisters.

Asher helped everyone get their lines in the water. Not five minutes later, Professor Kotz caught the first fish. Everly was stunned by how fiercely the fish fought. The professor was hard-pressed to keep hold of the fishing pole. When Asher netted the fish, they were all shocked by how small it was and how fiercely it had struggled. Asher had to be careful removing the hook from its mouth because of the razor-sharp teeth. He wore protective gloves.

The rest of them stared at the fish. Everly had seen drawings of piranha but was stunned to see one alive—well, almost alive. It was all mouth and teeth. A shiver ran down her spine, knowing how dangerous they could be.

In one of Asher's lectures, he'd reviewed the ten most dangerous types of wildlife in the Amazon. She didn't remember where piranha landed, but the fish was definitely one of the top five. The poisonous snakes and the wandering spider were also on that list.

Janice caught the second fish, and, like the professor, struggled to bring it close enough to the watercraft for Asher to net it. Once it had been freed from the line and placed in the cooler with the first fish, she beamed with pride.

"See, David? I told you I didn't need any help."

"Of course, my love. I'm proud of you."

For the next half hour, they all caught fish, Everly included. She'd done a little fishing as a kid. She didn't have the patience for it and didn't find it nearly as relaxing as her dad and brothers did. Her two sisters felt the same as Everly.

When she'd hooked the first piranha, she'd held her own and, like Janice, was quite proud of herself. Before long she caught a second and then a third. After her third catch, she retired her pole, leaned back, and enjoyed the afternoon. For once it wasn't raining, which was a rare treat. It rained every day without fail, but between cloudbursts there were moments of sunshine and warmth. They'd hit this fishing expedition at exactly the right time.

The Zodiac drifted beneath a row of vegetation along the bank, the current placing the watercraft in the shadows. After sitting in the hot sun for the last thirty minutes, the cool shade was welcome.

Everly closed her eyes, her head raised toward the sky, and soaked in the peace. Miriam Kotz was the only one who had yet to hook a fish, and Everly knew Asher didn't want to head back to the ship until everyone had experienced at least one catch.

Half asleep, Everly was startled awake when Miriam let loose with a piercing scream.

Everly bolted to an upright position.

Then Janice screamed.

Then she saw it.

A snake.

Not just any snake. This one was huge.

Apparently, it had fallen from the overhead foliage and landed in the middle of the Zodiac . . . directly in front of her.

Terrified, Everly gasped and leaped to her feet. The bottom of the Zodiac was wet and slippery, and she quickly lost her balance. With her arms flailing, she stumbled backward. Before she could right herself, she fell over the side of the raft and into the murky waters of the Amazon River.

CHAPTER TEN

Asher watched as Daisy lost her balance, arms thrashing, and flew backward out of the Zodiac into the piranha-infested water. With his heart in a wild panic, he immediately jumped into action. He grabbed hold of the snake, tossed it over the other side of the watercraft, and then leaned over the fat lip of the Zodiac, stretching out both arms to reach for Daisy.

Thanks to her life vest, she immediately bobbed to the surface, sputtering and frantically slapping the water in a crazed effort to reach him.

"Give me your arms," he shouted, almost in danger of slipping into the river himself.

David Brown gripped on to Asher's ankles as he lunged for Daisy, snatching hold of one of her wrists. With effort, he was able to drag her close enough to take hold of her other hand. Straining, Asher lifted her out of the water and back into the boat.

"Daisy," he cried, unable to keep the alarm out of his voice. "Dear God in heaven, are you all right?"

With her long hair dripping mercilessly onto her face and algae clinging to her clothing, Daisy tried to sit upright. Needing to know she hadn't been injured, Asher ran his hands down the length of her arms and then her legs until she slapped him away.

"I'm fine," she choked out, coughing up a mouthful of river water.

Asher slapped her back several times, hoping that would help.

"I swear I swallowed half the Amazon," she muttered, once she'd caught her breath. Using both hands, she brushed the hair away from her face and started trembling violently.

Then, to his horror, Daisy started to cry, big gulping sobs that shook her shoulders.

"Daisy, please, talk to me."

Her shoulders shook as she opened her mouth to speak and then closed it again.

Not knowing what to do, Asher looked to Janice Brown, hoping the older woman would have an inkling of what was the matter. Daisy didn't appear to have been injured. The worst that had happened was swallowing the river water.

Janice Brown scooted close to Daisy and placed her arm around her shoulders, not seeming to care that she was getting soaked herself. "It's all right, Daisy, let it out."

"You don't understand."

"What don't I understand?" the sympathetic older woman cooed.

"I'm not like this. I'm capable and strong . . . yet from the moment I stepped on board this cruise I have made a fool of myself," she blubbered between sobs. "I'm a complete klutz!"

"What you don't see, Daisy," Janice said, her words comforting and gentle, "is that you have endeared yourself to all of us. The things that have happened to you could have happened to any one of us."

"Maybe, but they happened to me."

Daisy sniffled several times and looked at Asher as if to tell him how sorry she was. Janice scooted back to join her husband.

Unable to resist, Asher gathered her in his arms, holding her against him as if he never intended to let her go. With the life jacket it was hard to get as close as he wanted to. Not that Asher cared if comforting her soaked his own clothes. Nothing was going to keep her out of his arms.

With his forehead braced against hers, he said, "I lost ten years off my life seeing you go overboard."

Daisy wiped her forearm under her nose. "Where's the snake?"

"Gone."

"Good thing, or I'd go back into the water," she said between sniffles, and made a gallant effort to smile.

He had to assume she was joking. It was hard to release her, but he needed to get her back to the ship. She was wet and miserable, and seeing her so uncomfortable made him even more eager to see her safely back to where she could shower and change.

Asher kept close watch over her as they zoomed at full speed across the river. Daisy shivered with shock and cold. She was a pitiful sight, sitting on the bottom of the Zodiac with her arms wrapped around her knees, water still dripping and pooling all around her.

Asher knew that piranha had a bad reputation, no thanks to Hollywood. The facts said differently. The fish rarely attacked humans. Furthermore, this area on the Amazon where they'd been fishing had an abundant supply of insects, crustaceans, worms, and seeds, which was their common diet, so Daisy was never in any real danger. Instinctively, he knew all that, and still, seeing her fall out of the Zodiac had panicked him.

Janice patted Daisy's hand and talked soothingly to her until they reached the ship. Asher radioed ahead to be sure there were towels waiting.

Daisy held back and was the last one off the Zodiac, and Asher personally helped her disembark and then walked her to her stateroom.

"Take a shower and then meet me," he said, finding it difficult to leave her.

With the towel wrapped around her shoulders, she sniffled. "I've already taken my allotted two showers for this week."

"It's fine, these are extenuating circumstances." He would never say it aloud, but Daisy looked like the Creature from the Black Lagoon. Although he was likely to be seen by both passenger and crew, he leaned forward to kiss her forehead. "I'll be waiting."

"I . . . I won't be long."

Surprising him, she leaned forward and pressed her head against his chest. "I don't know how I'm going to be able to look anyone in the eye."

"What makes you say that?"

"I'm such a klutz," she said and groaned. "I have been my entire life. No one wanted me on their teams in school. The only B grade I ever got was in PE."

"Daisy, love, no one is going to blame you for what happened, least of all me." She was adorable, dripping hair, soggy clothes, algae sticking out of her shoes. As odd as it might seem, he'd never seen anyone more beautiful than Daisy at that moment. He felt doubly protective of her and realized how much he'd come to care about her in such a short amount of time.

All too soon they'd go their separate ways, which was good and bad. Good because it was becoming incredibly easy to fall in love with this woman. Their differences weren't going to change, though, so the sooner she was gone, the better. And bad because he knew she was going to haunt him for a good long while.

Asher wandered into the meeting room, poured himself a cup of coffee from the ever-ready pot, and grabbed an oatmeal cookie, still warm from the oven. The cooking staff supplied an abundance of snacks that were available all day. A few of the other passengers had returned from the fishing expedition and were sitting around visiting. He enjoyed watching those on board socialize with one another. He knew friendships were often formed on these cruises. It wasn't unusual for couples to meet and then travel together on another Explorer ship at a future date.

"Asher," one of the passengers named Penny called to him. She was around fifty and had been appropriately named, as her hair was the color of freshly minted copper, now streaked with gray. "What's this I hear about Daisy falling overboard? Was she hurt? What in heaven's name happened?"

He explained about the snake and assured the other woman that all was well and that thankfully Daisy was no worse for wear.

"That poor girl; it seems everything happens to her."

"It certainly seems that way, doesn't it? Although I don't think she welcomed any of what's happened. I have to say she's been a good sport about it all."

Penny nodded. "From what I heard, this wasn't exactly the cruise she'd been expecting."

"So I understand." Asher liked to think it was fate that had brought her to the Amazon Explorer. He didn't have all the details straight in his mind as to how the misunderstanding had happened, but it seemed to have something to do with an overeager young assistant. Whatever had gone wrong had been in his favor. He would never have met her otherwise.

Fifteen minutes after he dropped Daisy at her stateroom, she entered the main meeting area. Her gaze immediately caught his. "If you'll excuse me, I want to check on Daisy."

"Of course," Penny said with an easy smile.

Daisy had showered and changed clothes, but she wore a forlorn look as she entered the room. Asher met her and reached for her hand, leading her into the small alcove where they'd sat before.

"How are you feeling?" he asked. Once they were seated side by side, he reached for her free hand, holding both of hers in his.

She lowered her gaze and seemed to be concentrating on their joined hands. "I feel like such an idiot to have overreacted to that snake."

"You can't blame yourself, Daisy. That could have happened to anyone."

"You keep saying that, but it happened to me. I saw that

snake and panicked, and then I lost my balance and couldn't stop my momentum. Before I knew it, I was in the water. I don't know what's wrong with me. This isn't me. I'm not like this in the office. I'm capable, and mature . . . or I used to be. I hardly know myself any longer. It feels like my entire world has been turned upside down."

He raised her hand to his lips and kissed her knuckles. "I know. I haven't been myself since the moment we met. I knew that it was highly unlikely that the piranhas would attack you, yet all that science and knowledge flew out the proverbial window the instant you fell overboard." Asher hated to admit that he'd been terrified. It'd taken everything inside him not to jump into the river after her.

Her cheeks flushed a fetching shade of pink.

"If any harm had come to you, I don't know what I would have done. I couldn't have handled it." Even now, just remembering her catapulting out of the Zodiac skyrocketed his heart rate.

"All's well that ends well, right?"

The captain appeared and made the rounds, greeting passengers and making small talk. It was part of Asher's duty to mingle with the passengers as time would allow. He reluctantly dropped her hand. He didn't want to leave her, but he didn't want to ignore his position with the team, either.

"Go," Daisy whispered, as if understanding his dilemma.

Asher noticed that the captain was making small talk with the Browns and joined them.

Janice smiled as her husband continued with the story. "And overboard she went. Good thing Asher kept his wits about him. Both Janice and I were frozen. We didn't know what to do."

"You did help, dear," Janice reminded him.

"He did," Asher said. "David helped me pull Ms. Lancaster out of the river."

"Ms. Lancaster," Captain Martin repeated, slowly shaking his head. "I should have known it was her. She seems to have a talent for trouble."

Asher had to agree, although none of what happened was anything but coincidence.

"Thankfully, the cruise ends in a few days and she'll be disembarking."

A day Asher both dreaded and welcomed.

"I'd best check on the young woman myself," the captain continued, as the Browns left. He frowned and added, "The company would frown upon a lawsuit."

"I don't believe Ms. Lancaster has any intention of taking legal action," Asher assured him.

"That's good to hear."

When he glanced over to where Daisy had been sitting, he saw that she was gone. He could only assume she'd returned to her stateroom. As tempting as it was to check on her, he resisted. At first, he'd been determined to keep out of her way, but it seemed the universe was drawing them together.

His attempts to avoid her had been a miserable failure

and he'd felt he had to explain himself. Now he felt closer to her than ever. The last thing he intended when they'd met the night before was to kiss her again. She'd asked where they were headed now. Asher wished he knew. One thing was certain: If he let her weave her way into his heart, this relationship was guaranteed to fail. Outside of this attraction, their lives had shockingly little in common.

He knew it.

She knew it.

They were both smart people who recognized the odds of making anything come of this shipboard romance. Nevertheless, this attraction they battled seemed electric. Every time they were together, Asher found himself smiling. He genuinely liked Daisy as a person.

Furthermore, he strongly suspected she was a different person in Chicago than the woman he had come to know in the Amazon. It would be far better for him to hold on to the memory of her as he knew her now. In Chicago she was Everly, confident, capable, and savvy, but here in the Amazon with him, she was Daisy, lovable, funny, and disaster-prone. Daisy was the woman he was attracted to, and he wasn't sure he would feel the same way about Everly.

When the time came, he'd bid her farewell, put her out of his mind, and move on with his life.

So why did he feel like forgetting Daisy was going to be much harder than he wanted to accept?

CHAPTER ELEVEN

The last days of the cruise flew by far too quickly to suit Everly. As part of the itinerary, the Amazon Explorer took a tributary off the Amazon River that led the ship back to the port in Manaus.

Janice and David Brown were staying on for an additional week and trekking deep into the rainforest to stay in an elaborate tree house. Everly had to give Janice credit; the older woman was willing to follow her husband to the ends of the earth and was determined to experience every adventure with him.

The cruise had been far and away better than Everly could ever have anticipated, and that was due in a huge part to Asher. She'd learned more about the fragile ecosystem of the rainforest and experienced adventures that would last her a lifetime. But it was only a small part of what had made this trip such a success. Everly had made good friends with the Browns and the Kotzes. Professor Kotz promised on their next trip to the States, they would visit America's Windy City and connect with Daisy.

The one drawback was that she'd be leaving Asher behind. On the flight in, Everly had dreamed of finding a Latin lover, never expecting that she would meet a man who would turn her world upside down. Now that she knew Asher, she didn't want their connection to end with the cruise. She'd done a lot of thinking in the last two weeks. Thinking about her position with Easy Home. Thinking about her relationship with her family. And a whole lot of thinking about Asher.

Everly knew she was falling in love with him. It excited her and terrified her at the same time. Meeting him had changed her. The whole world felt fresh and new. The sun seemed brighter, the stars clearer. Everly longed to wrap this feeling around her like a thick winter sweater and hold it tight against her heart.

She wanted to believe Asher felt the same. The way he kissed her said he did. Yet several times over the course of the last week, he'd insinuated that whatever it was between them wasn't sustainable, implying that at the end of the cruise she would leave, and she'd never hear from him again.

Now that the ship was nearing the port in Manaus, Everly

knew she couldn't do it. If she was truly never going to be with Asher again, then she needed to speak up and tell him how she felt. She'd survived a negative reaction to a mosquito bite, been lost in the jungle with fierce Amazon warriors, and fallen into piranha-infested waters, but telling Asher that she was falling in love with him felt scarier than anything she'd endured while on this trip.

Bolstering her courage, she reminded herself that if he felt anything close to what she did, he'd be willing to give this romance a chance. She'd been in the business world too long to ignore the fact that if there was a will there was a way. Though it might sound clichéd, experience told her it wasn't.

Asher might not admit it, but she was convinced that deep down he wanted her to remain in his life as badly as she wanted to be in his. He couldn't have kissed her the way he did if this was nothing more than a shipboard fling. Those toe-curling kisses sparked hope that he'd recognized whatever it was that held him back and agree they needed to give this . . . whatever it was . . . a shot.

The Amazon Explorer arrived at the port in Manaus at eight that morning, and once the vessel had been cleared by the port authorities, they were told they should be able to disembark at around ten.

Asher sat with her in their favorite spot, the alcove in the main gathering room, and held her hand. Other passengers mingled about, chatting and sharing photographs. The Browns were chatting with Penny, and Professor Kotz spoke to Mike, the safety officer.

It was now or never. She'd either speak up and tell Asher how she felt or walk away and regret it for the rest of her life.

Her heart was pounding so hard it echoed in her ears, cutting out all ambient conversations.

"There's something I need to tell you, Asher," she said, gathering her courage.

Something in her voice must have alerted him to the fact that she was serious. His eyes locked with hers.

Laying her heart before him, she said, "I'm falling in love with you . . . I know we have only known each other two weeks. But they have been two of the most wonderful weeks of my life, and I don't want them to end. I know there are obstacles in our way, and questions we need to answer, compromises that we'll need to make. I'm willing, so willing, and I hope you are, too."

Her big declaration was met with stark silence. It felt like all the air had been vacuumed out of the room by a giant hose and as if the sun had sunk low in the sky, taking the warmth and the light with it.

When Asher did speak, his voice was low and regretful. "You're not actually falling in love with me, Daisy."

She shook her head, denying his words. "I know my own heart."

"You might think you do," he said. "These shipboard romances are pretty common. After watching what happens with other members of the crew, I know these feelings quickly fade. By the time you're back in the office and settle into your routine, I'll be a distant memory."

She was about to argue, but Asher abruptly changed the subject. "You are ready to get back to the office, aren't you?" he asked, as if he hadn't heard a word she'd said. "I can only imagine how many hundreds of emails you have waiting for you to answer."

Embarrassed that he'd responded to her declaration with comments about emails, she stared back at him. She was about to speak when Alex Freeman and his wife strolled past with suitcases in hand. He paused when he saw Everly sitting with Asher.

"I hope despite your adventures you enjoyed the cruise, Daisy."

"I did, and thank you." She noticed his suitcases. "Are you off for the holidays?"

Alex frowned at Asher. "The entire crew is. The ship is going through maintenance, so we have two weeks free. Alice and I are heading to Rio for some Christmas fun."

"The entire crew?" she asked. Asher hadn't mentioned having any free time. This changed everything.

Alex strode off and Everly turned to Asher, excitement churning in her like an oil rig gusher. "Asher," she said, tightening her hold around his hands. "Fly back with me. You said your brother has been wanting you to visit. And Chicago at Christmastime . . . It's magical. All the lights and the festivities. And you can meet my family and taste my Grandma Ruth's recipe for fudge. You like fudge, don't you? Everyone does."

Asher pulled his hand free. "I won't be going to Chicago."

"But . . ." She didn't finish as it hit her like running face-first into a brick wall. Asher hadn't wanted her to know about this break in his schedule. He'd purposely not told her.

If Asher thought she would ignore this, he was wrong. "You have a whole two weeks free, and—"

"Daisy, please," he said stiffly, cutting her off. "Don't do this."

"Don't do what?" she asked, her brain working at laser speed. She refused to believe he didn't share her feelings. He was lying. He had to be. He'd insisted he wasn't one to play with her heart, that he didn't routinely fall into romantic relationships. She was the exception. And she'd believed him. He'd been sincere. Honest. He couldn't have held her and kissed her without experiencing even a small part of what she did.

Shifting uncomfortably, Asher looked away as if he wasn't sure what to say next. He'd put his foot in a big pile of regret and didn't know how to back out of it without making an even bigger mess.

"I think you're wonderful, Daisy, and I've grown fond of you."

"You're fond of me?" She hated that word. Fond. It sounded weak. Watered-down affection. He liked her the same way he liked dessert following dinner. Sparingly. In small doses.

Asher lowered his head as if the words were as difficult for him to say as they were for her to hear.

An awkward silence stretched between them as thick as concrete. Everly found it difficult to breathe.

Asher refused to look at her.

When she found she could speak again, she said, "I guess this means that everything you said was a lie—"

"No," he said, cutting her off, "I meant every single word. Please accept that it's better this way."

"Better for whom? Better for you? Better for me?"

Squaring his shoulders, he looked at her then, his gaze intense. "You'll go back to Chicago and be Everly again. I don't know that woman, and I'm not entirely sure I would even like her."

She flinched at his words. "I'm one and the same person, Asher. It doesn't matter if I'm standing in front of hundreds of real estate brokers or milking the family cow. I can't be anyone else but me . . . the very woman you're looking at."

"And I can't be anyone else but myself," he fired back. "I don't fit in your world and you don't fit in mine."

He stared at her, his eyes intense and full of regret, as though pleading with her to understand.

"We could both try to keep these feelings alive, attempt a long-distance relationship," he continued. "You in Chicago and me down here. We could write letters, email and text or video-chat when possible, even manage a few trips back and forth. But to what end?"

Everly opened her mouth, prepared to answer. Asher wasn't finished, though, and seemed to have a lot more to say.

"A few weeks, months, maybe even a year from now, one of us would recognize the futility of it all. It might seem cruel to let you go now with nothing more than what we had these last two weeks. But eventually either you or I will accept that the only viable answer is to walk away. By doing it now, I'm saving us both the angst and heartache."

Clenching her hands together to the point that she cut off the blood supply to her fingers, she glared at him. "Forgive me, Asher, I thought we had something special. I was wrong. These two weeks were nothing more than an enjoyable romantic interlude . . . as you said, a shipboard romance. I apologize for putting more into it than warranted."

He looked away, as if struggling not to contradict her.

She faked a short laugh. "I blame all those silly romance books I read. That must be the problem."

"How's that?"

"How?" she repeated. "Those books led me to believe in happy endings. This is the real world, so please forgive me for being silly and looking for more. It's clear you don't have more to give. It's unfortunate, too, because I do. You could have had my heart so easily."

"Daisy, you think this is easy? I'm never going to forget you."

She didn't believe him. Out of sight, out of mind. That was what he was hoping for, and she didn't doubt he would make it happen. "Nice of you to say. I, on the other hand, am going to put the full force of my will and determination toward forgetting I ever met you. It's what you want, and as you've said, it's for the best."

He paled but didn't disagree.

"Before I leave the ship, I want to thank you. When I arrived, I was overworked, overstressed, and strung out. I'm not any longer, and it's due to the lessons I learned from being with you. Seeing nature through your eyes was a beautiful experience."

"Thank you."

In another day, Everly would be back in Chicago and Asher would fill his time with whatever he had planned. What he didn't know was that she wouldn't return the same woman who'd left. The Amazon and Asher had changed her, and if for no other reason, she had him to thank for that.

After two weeks away Everly could see clearly where she

had veered off the path and become absorbed in work to the exclusion of everything else. Rescuing Jack, taking on responsibilities that were meant to be shared, had cost her far more than she'd realized. It was only when she'd had time to clear her head, and she'd had plenty of that while down with that fever, trapped in her stateroom, that a curtain had lifted, a fog had dissipated, and she could see the woman she had become. It had been eye-opening, to say the least. Everly discovered she didn't want to be that woman any longer. She had a new set of priorities, and once she was back, one of the first things she intended to do was enlighten Jack.

Before long it was time to leave the ship. Asher chose to skip over their awkward conversation.

"What time is your flight?" he asked.

She told him, and reached for her suitcase when Asher stepped up and tried to take it himself.

"I'll get that. Thanks anyway." It was a matter of pride that she carry it herself.

"It's a shame you never had a chance to visit the opera house or the fish market," he said, as if looking for nonsensical ways to fill the silence.

"Maybe next time," she said, her voice devoid of emotion. She had to wonder if she'd ever return to Brazil. She hadn't seen much of the country, other than the rainforest and the Amazon River. In her present state of mind, she preferred to avoid any place that would remind her of Asher.

"The varieties of fish in the market are something to behold," Asher continued, as if delivering one of his lectures. "The Amazon has the largest number of freshwater fish in the world, with more than fifty-six hundred species."

His commentary did little to fill the silence. She stood in line, waiting to disembark, looking out at the row of taxis. Within minutes she would walk away from Asher and it would be the end, just the way he wanted.

He went down the gangway with her, something she hadn't expected him to do, and led her toward the row of cabs. He spoke to the first one in line in fluent Portuguese. The driver nodded and stepped out of the vehicle before taking her luggage and placing it in the trunk.

"I guess this is it," Asher said. He stood in front of her, his hands resting gently on her shoulders.

Everly broke the contact and stepped back. It had taken this long for her fighting spirit to ignite. "Are you seriously going to let me walk away, Asher?"

He blinked as though her words shocked him. It was clear that as far as he was concerned, this matter had already been settled.

"We've already been through this, Daisy. I'm saving us—"

"Don't say 'us,' because this is your decision, this is all about you. I don't know what happened in your past that makes you afraid to fall in love. Whatever it was must be a doozy."

He shook his head. "You're wrong."

"I very well could be. What I know now is that you're not the man I thought you were, Asher Adams. You're a coward."

He flinched and retreated a step.

"One day you're going to look back and remember that you walked away from a woman who would love you with all her heart. A woman who would welcome you into her world and be willing to share yours, only you were afraid to take the chance. You shoved her away, giving in to your fears and deciding what was best for her without giving her a say or caring enough to make the effort. Have a good life, Asher. I suspect it will be lonely and empty. Just remember it was by your own choice."

Having had her say, she climbed into the backseat of the taxi and closed the door. No sooner had she taken her seat when the cab pulled away from the dock.

Everly didn't look back.

This really was the end. She told Asher she intended to put him out of her mind, and she meant it.

By the time Everly landed in Chicago, she'd been awake nearly nineteen hours. Going from the airport to her condo in the middle of the night was smooth sailing with a complete lack of traffic. Everly noticed the signs of Christmas everywhere. As she drove past Navy Pier, the bright lights shone a welcome home.

Checking her phone, she saw that Jack had sent her multiple messages, asking her to stop by the office as soon as she could. This didn't surprise her. She wondered how he'd survived the last two weeks and hoped he'd been able to deal with whatever crisis had come up, because she fully intended to head to Indiana as soon as possible.

As she thumbed through the text messages, she realized she'd been looking for one from Asher and wanted to kick herself for her romantic heart. He had her phone number, as he'd promised to forward several photos. Since he hadn't reached out, she had to believe that really had been a final good-bye.

Everly had a decision to make. She could be thankful for the time they had and move forward, or she could wallow in the loss of the most promising relationship she'd ever experienced. She knew what she had to do and was determined to make it happen.

The following morning, after showering and unpacking, she headed to the office, as requested. Several of the staff greeted her and commented that it was good to have her back.

She noticed Annette wasn't at her desk and wondered where she was. Perhaps with Everly away, the assistant had really shown her true colors and hadn't bothered to show up for work until she felt like it.

"Everly." Jack rushed out of his office as soon as he saw her. "You're here. Did you get my texts? I have to say it hasn't been quite the same around here with you gone. I need you to—"

"Where's Annette?" she asked, cutting him off.

"Annette . . . Can we talk about her later?"

"No. I need to square something with her."

"I know, I know," Jack said, his face filled with regret. "I learned what she did. I asked her to book you a luxury cruise so you could relax and recharge, and instead she sent you sailing down the Amazon."

"It was a dirty trick." Everly didn't want Jack to know the cruise had turned into the experience of a lifetime.

Jack shifted his weight from one foot to the other. "I believe she regretted that after you'd left."

That was a surprise. "Did she admit what she'd done?"

"No . . . not exactly."

"Then how'd you find out?"

Obviously uneasy, Jack rubbed the side of his face. "Accounts Payable questioned the expense, and when I saw that Annette had booked you on the Amazon Explorer, I asked her about it. She admitted she thought it was only fair because you were a terrible boss who was demanding, critical, and unfair."

"And you believed her?"

"No. I put her to work on another project, which she mishandled. No one in the office was willing to work with her, so I sent her home to think of a way she could improve her attitude."

Everly had to resist laughing out loud. "Did that work?"

Jack's shoulders slumped. "As expected, she went crying to her mother, who then called and berated me for mistreating her precious daughter."

Everly crossed her arms. This was getting better by the minute.

"My sister said she didn't feel I'd been fair to Annette and that I had made her the assistant to a tyrant."

"What?" Everly exploded.

"And then Louise said that Annette would no longer be working for me and would seek employment elsewhere."

That was rich. "In which case, it all worked out."

"I suppose, except my sister is no longer speaking to me."

Everly suspected Annette wouldn't be able to hold down any job for long, with that attitude. Both mother and daughter were in for a rude awakening. That would come in time.

"You said you wanted to see me?" Everly asked. She had no intention of staying in the office for more than an hour or two, if that.

He nodded enthusiastically. "Would you mind stopping by my office? There are a fair number of items I need you to review."

"What items?" she asked, crossing her arms tightly over

her torso, nonverbally letting him know she had no intention of jumping to the rescue.

Her partner immediately started a long list of problems that had arisen in the two weeks she'd been away. After about ten minutes, Everly stopped him. "Jack, if you remember, I am taking off the entire month of December. I'm not giving up the next two weeks solving problems you should've been handling while I was away."

Jack responded as if he hadn't heard her. "Of course . . . you're probably jet-lagged. This won't take more than a day or two to clear up."

She shook her head. "You're not hearing me, Jack. I'm heading to Indiana to spend time with my family. Unless the entire company is in jeopardy, I suggest you manage what-ever comes up. You and the team can do this. You don't need me leaping to the rescue."

His mouth sagged open in shock.

Everly gently patted his cheek.

"But . . . But, Everly, I waited for your return. I thought you'd be the best one to handle this situation."

She wasn't giving in. "I'm sure whatever it is, you'll figure it out." She smiled and headed out of the office, deciding to catch up on emails from her condo.

It felt good to resist getting trapped in the office her first day back. If there was anything truly serious that demanded her attention, then the team would reach out.

Once home, she sorted through what felt like a thousand

emails. With less than two weeks to go before Christmas, Everly was anxious to get to Indiana and her family. She'd missed everyone far more than she realized. Her hope was that she could do a little Christmas shopping with her two sisters and hang out with her nieces and nephews. It'd been way too long since they'd had quality time together.

If there was enough snow on the ground, perhaps she could convince her father to bring out the big sleigh that had been in the family for a couple of generations. Those sleigh rides were some of her happiest Christmas memories.

It was after five when Jack called her cell. "Will you be in the office tomorrow?" he asked, sounding anxious.

"No!"

"No?" Jack repeated. "Everly, I don't think you realize the seriousness of the situation."

"You're CEO. You can take care of it." Seeing that she'd checked in with the team and not one of them had mentioned anything that dire, she had to believe Jack was exaggerating, which was something he tended to do.

Silence followed, and she was about to disconnect when Jack spoke, his tone urgent. "You've changed."

"Yes," she agreed, "I have."

"Is it because I refused to listen to you about Annette?"

"That was only part of it. You were right, Jack. I didn't appreciate how right you were until I got away from the office for more than a day or two," she said.

Jack laughed. "What exactly was I right about?"

"Me. I was stressed out and badly in need of a vacation. I learned quite a bit about myself while I was away, and as a result, I'd like to suggest a few changes."

"What sort of changes?" he asked, concern coating the question.

Everly outlined the various promotions and reallocating of responsibilities among the staff, convinced he wasn't going to like her suggestions. To her surprise, he agreed to all her recommendations. Her workload would be lightened, giving her the life she hoped to carve out for a future.

"From now on, I expect you to carry your share of the business. I won't be working more than a forty-hour week."

"Forty hours. You? I've never met anyone more ambitious than you are. You spend more time in this office than anyone. What's changed?"

Asher's face flashed before her and she frowned. "Not what, Jack, but who. It's me who changed. Me."

CHAPTER TWELVE

Everly drove down the long, frozen dirt driveway that led to the Lancaster family farm. Cheerful Christmas carols played from her car's stereo. Despite the uplifting music, she was in a somber mood. Although she'd been determined to put Asher out of her mind, he clung to her thoughts like Velcro. Everly had been back only four days, although it felt more like four weeks.

Deep down, she wanted to believe he would have a change of heart, mainly because that was what she hoped for her own selfish reasons. It disturbed her that he could connect with her if he wanted to. Obviously, he didn't. He had her phone number after sharing several photos with her, so it would be a simple matter to send a text. He could have asked if she'd made it home safely. He hadn't because she was out of his mind. She'd best accept his decision and move on. Asher had. When she thought of him, she was filled with a sense of loss, of what might have been if he'd been brave enough to give them a shot.

Once she'd parked by the old barn, Jasper, their family dog, wandered out, his long tail slapping against his hind quarters. He was a Great Pyrenees and was a wonderful farm dog, especially around the chickens her mother raised, the horses, and the few head of cattle her father kept for beef.

She hadn't climbed completely out of the car before the back door opened and her mother flew down the porch steps. "Daisy!" Lois Lancaster cried, racing over with her arms wide open. "I didn't think you'd ever get here."

The two embraced and Everly noticed her mother had tears in her eyes. "It's about time you came home."

"It is," Everly agreed.

"Let's get you out of the cold." With their arms around each other's waists, they walked back into the house.

Her mother had always made the most of the Christmas season. The tree was up and decorated, taking over an entire corner of the living room. The decorations hadn't changed through the years, though more had been added until there was barely a tree limb without two or three ornaments. The kitchen was rich with the scent of a roast in the Crock-Pot and freshly baked sugar cookies spread across the kitchen counter, awaiting frosting and decorations.

Christmas cards from family and friends were taped along the sides of the doorway that led into the dining room. The mistletoe hung in the archway between the two rooms the way it had every Christmas for as long as she could remember. She smiled as her gaze wandered around the living area, where there were several Nativity scenes. And then she looked to the fireplace where seven stockings hung, the same as when she was a little girl, as she knew they would.

This was home and this was her family. Everly wrapped the comfort of all that was familiar around her like a well-loved sweater.

Dressed in his coveralls, her father rose from his recliner and hugged her close. "About time, girl. You've been away too long."

"I have, but I'm here now and I don't intend to leave until well after Christmas," she promised, and kissed his weathered cheek.

"Good." He gave her a gentle squeeze, then looked to his wife of forty years. "How much longer before dinner?"

"All in good time. Rose and her family are coming."

He nodded approvingly.

"Lily is bringing dessert later."

Everly couldn't ask for a better homecoming. Her family was working overtime to make sure she felt welcome, and Everly appreciated that they made the effort.

"What about Jeff and John?" Her twin brothers lived half

a mile down the road. The two had always been inseparable and had built homes next door to each other.

"They'll be here tomorrow night; said they didn't want to overwhelm you the first night home."

"Snow is predicted for tonight," her father said from behind his newspaper. "Thought I'd hitch up the sleigh sometime before Christmas, give the grandkids a ride."

"The grandkids?" Everly protested with a large grin. "What about me?"

"You can come if you want."

"I do." Riding in the sleigh was one of her favorite Christmas traditions.

"I'll have cookies and cocoa waiting for you when you return," her mother promised.

Everly couldn't believe she'd missed Christmas with her family the year before because of work. At some point over the last few years she'd lost sight of her priorities. It'd been a gradual shift and had started in small ways, culminating with Christmas. She'd told herself heading to the farm for the holidays would be a distraction and she needed to focus on the business. It didn't help that she felt like the odd man out most of the time. She was different from her siblings: her sense of drive, her need to excel and be the best. Like her father had often said, she had the middle-child syndrome. With everyone together in the same room, the noise level rivaled that of the cheering crowd at an NFL football game.

Much of the time Everly felt that she was on the outside looking in rather than being involved. She wasn't sure who was to blame and was beginning to think this feeling was more on her than the rest of the family. One thing she could never deny was the abundance of love. A love she was only now fully appreciating.

When suffering from the reaction to the mosquito bite, Everly had wanted her mother. It made her smile now. She was hurting so much from Asher's rejection and felt relief to have her mother close, although she had no intention of mentioning him. She wasn't looking for sympathy as much as comfort.

Everly carried her suitcase up the well-worn staircase to the bedroom she'd shared with her two sisters. Three single beds had been crammed into the larger of the two bedrooms, with barely enough space to maneuver between them. Each sister had one chest of drawers with a lone closet that they were forced to section off into thirds. The five kids were required to share the one bathroom. Jeff and John swore they learned to dance, waiting for their turn. She could laugh about it now, but at the time, juggling for privacy had been a festering thorn in her flesh. When she'd complained, her mother had insisted sharing with her siblings produced character. Perhaps it had and created other skills besides, like putting on her makeup in under five minutes.

As she walked down the stairs, she heard the back door open off the kitchen.

"Daisy, where are you?" Rose shouted. "Get your butt down here."

Yup, her family wanted to be sure she felt welcomed. Everly couldn't remember the last time her oldest sister had shown any real enthusiasm at her visits. Everly left her room and came down the steps. She didn't have a chance to breathe before her sister grabbed her into a bear hug. "Missed you, girl."

Everly hugged her back.

Rose, her sister, the hairstylist, held her at arm's length. "Hmm," she said carefully, studying Everly. "When was the last time you had a haircut?"

Everly grinned. "It's been a while."

"You're telling me! We're sitting you in my chair. Be ready when I call you. I'm taking scissors to that mop you've got going on."

"Okay, okay," Everly said, sighing. No way was she telling her sister she'd spent a hundred dollars for this haircut a short week before leaving for Brazil.

The three women dished up the pot roast, mashed potatoes, gravy, corn, and coleslaw and set it on the table while Rose's husband, Stan, and her father talked local politics. Russell and little Rosie played with Jasper, who lovingly ate up the attention.

Conversation over the dinner table rarely lagged while she was a kid, and that hadn't changed. Questions flew at her about her time in South America. Knowing her dad would enjoy hearing about her fishing for piranha, she went into detail about how fiercely the fish fought. She didn't mention taking a tumble into the Amazon River. Both her father and brother-in-law were suitably impressed.

"Aunt Daisy, Aunt Daisy," Russell said, vying for her attention. "How did the piranha taste?"

She looked toward her young nephew. "It was good eating."

"Did you swallow any teeth?"

"Nope, but those teeth were scary-looking." Reaching for her phone, she brought up a photo Asher had shared with her, revealing the piranha with its mouth open and dominated by huge rows of teeth. When she passed the photo to the nine-year-old, his eyes got as big as dinner plates.

"Dad," he cried, "look." He glanced toward Everly. "Aunt Daisy, do you think you could take me fishing on the Amazon one day?"

"Russell," Rose admonished.

"Maybe," Everly told him. "You never know. My guess is that if you want to travel to Brazil, you'll be able to find your own way when the time comes."

He smiled as if she'd handed him a plane ticket. "Do you really think so?"

"You can do anything you put your mind and your heart to," she assured him.

"I don't want to go to the Amazon to fish for piranha," six-year-old Rosie said. "I'd rather go to Disney World in Florida."

Rose nudged Everly's foot and winked, silently letting her know that the little girl was going to get her wish.

"Christmas?" Everly asked under her breath.

"Right after," her sister mouthed back.

Following dinner, Rosie wanted Everly to read her a story. She felt guilty leaving the cleanup to her mother and sister, but they were quick to usher her out the door. Rosie already had a book picked out. She handed it to Everly, who sat on the sofa, expecting Rosie to sit next to her. To her delight, the little girl climbed into her lap. This story was much loved, and it seemed Rosie had heard it many times. Before Everly finished, her sweet niece was fast asleep.

"Think it's time we head home," Stan said, motioning toward Rosie. He lifted his daughter into his arms while Rose helped get her daughter into her coat. The little one barely stirred.

"I don't want to go," Russell whined. "I want to stay here and hear more about the rainforest."

"And you will," Everly promised. "I'll be here all the way until the New Year. We'll go on a sleigh ride and build a snow fort and challenge your uncles to a snowball fight."

Russell nodded enthusiastically. "You promise?"

"I do," she said, as he hugged tight around her waist.

Everly kissed the top of his head. "Now head on home

and get lots of sleep and I'll print out some of the other photos I have from the Amazon." She knew he'd be excited when
he saw the giant lily pads and some of the other photos
Asher had sent through Dropbox.

Rose and her family left and not ten minutes later, Lily
appeared carrying a platter of traditional Christmas candies, the very ones they'd cooked with their grandmother
and mother through the years. Everly was heartened by the
way her family was going above and beyond to make sure she
knew she was welcome.

"Is that Grandma Ruth's fudge?" she asked.

"Is there any other?" Lily teased.

"And her divinity." Everly's weakness. "I have dreams
about this divinity."

"If you'd come home more, you could have your fill."

"Be quiet and give me a hug," Everly said, as she placed
the platter in the middle of the kitchen table. The two embraced, rocking back and forth with sisterly affection. As
teens they'd barely been able to tolerate each other. Now
they saw each other infrequently and their teenage squabbles
didn't seem to matter.

"Where are Jason and the boys?" their mother asked,
about Lily's husband and sons.

"Cub Scouts," she said, and then looked to Everly. "Jason's the scout leader or he'd be here. You'll get a chance to
see them all long before Christmas."

"Russell talked me into building a snow fort so he could

challenge Uncle Jeff and John to a snowball fight. I want your boys on our team." She couldn't throw worth a darn, but her nephew didn't know that.

The smell of freshly brewed coffee filled the kitchen as the three women sat around the table and chatted. Everly caught up with her sister and the family news. Jason worked for the fire department as a paramedic, and Lily worked part-time at the bakery.

When her two sisters had married young, Everly, intent on getting a college education, had assumed they were making a big mistake. Rose quit after her freshman year of college and then entered cosmetology school. Lily got her Liberal Arts degree before marrying. At the time it'd boggled Everly's mind that they hadn't been interested in continuing their education and all the opportunities that it would afford them.

By marrying young, neither of her sisters had experienced life. They'd both been eager to settle down and start their families. Rose and Lily were smart, achieving good grades in school, and could have gotten into any school they wanted to. Rose had met Stan while she was a college freshman and married only after finishing her cosmetology course. Lily married her high school sweetheart, the very boy she'd gone with to her junior and senior proms.

Everly had always felt like they had lost out on opportunities for independence and career success, but seeing and hearing about their lives with their families, she realized she was the one who'd lost out. She didn't regret her career; she enjoyed her work, but she'd allowed her drive and ambition to rule her life. She'd closed herself off from experiences and relationships in order to focus on the next innovation, the next opportunity. It was eye-opening to realize she'd cheated herself.

"You're really going to stay until the new year?" Lily pressed.

"I really am."

"What about Easy Home?"

Reaching for a second piece of fudge, Everly relaxed against the back of the kitchen chair. "The company will survive with or without me."

Her mother and Lily exchanged glances.

"What?" Everly asked, savoring the chocolate flavor of the fudge. Her grandmother's recipe called for cocoa and condensed milk and was a family favorite.

"You're different, Daisy," Lily said. "What changed?"

She hesitated, unsure how much to say, and then decided this was her family and it was useless to keep a secret from them. "While on the cruise, I had the chance to reassess a few of the choices I've made. It was enlightening, to say the least. My priorities have been out of whack. It was time to set them straight."

Lily sat up and shared a quick look with their mother. "You came up with this all on your own?"

She nodded.

"Was there a man involved?"

Her shock must have shown, because her sister nodded knowingly. Swallowing tightly, Everly forced a smile, which she was sure looked pitifully sad. "I'd prefer not to talk about it."

Her mother was instantly sympathetic. "Oh, sweetie, did he break your heart?"

"Mom, please." Everly tilted her head back to stare at the ceiling for fear the tears that welled in her eyes would spill down her cheeks. Since her return, Everly hadn't shed a tear. Now they flooded her eyes.

"I'm the foolish one to put credence on a shipboard romance," she whispered through the tightness in her throat. "He doesn't want me."

Silence followed as if neither her mother nor her sister believed any man wouldn't want Everly.

"Oh, honey, I'm so sorry."

Everly wiped the moisture from her face. "I'll survive. This isn't the first time I've been disappointed, and it won't be the last. Now, please, can we talk about something else?"

"Of course."

They all made a determined effort to move on and avoid talking about the one subject, the one person, Everly couldn't seem to forget.

CHAPTER THIRTEEN

Asher was forced to admit it. He was miserable. He hated that Daisy had learned about the ship's two-week maintenance break. The hurt and disappointment in her eyes when she realized he'd purposely withheld the information made his chest ache. He couldn't get the image of her shock out of his mind.

Foolishly, Asher assumed that once Daisy returned to the States, he'd be able to move on within a day or two. He didn't expect he'd be able to forget her, at least not right away, of course. It made sense that it would take time, time he was willing to wait out.

He had plans for the maintenance break. Plans to relax and explore a region of the rainforest interior he'd not been to before. His itinerary was set, but ultimately he couldn't dig up the enthusiasm to make the journey and at the last minute had bowed out and stayed behind.

A few days after Christmas he would be back on the river with a load of fresh passengers, eager for adventure and to learn and explore. Meeting a new slate of guests would help distract him and help take his mind off Daisy.

He would never be able to think of her as Everly. To him, she would always be Daisy. Everly was that dedicated business executive who had worked herself into a frazzle. Daisy was the lovable, klutzy, adorable . . . He stopped, finding himself doing it again: thinking of her and the closeness they'd shared.

Gritting his teeth to the point that his jaw ached, he forced her from his mind. Whatever she chose to call herself was of no concern to him.

Restless and bored, Asher ventured into town, found an Internet café, and wrote a long, newsy email to his parents, copying his brother. He mentioned his last cruise and went on about a woman he'd met and some of what had happened to her. Rereading his email, he realized nearly everything he'd written in one way or another was related to Daisy. He erased nearly all of it and sent a much condensed version.

It wasn't long before his mother responded.

Honestly, Asher, how long before you're ready to settle down? First it was Antarctica, then it was the Amazon.

Your father and I barely see you. Don't you think it's time you found a good woman, settled down, and gave your father and me grandchildren?

Asher read her short message and groaned. His mother was right, and he knew it. Most men his age had settled into marriage and were raising a family. But it wasn't like he was able to pluck a wife off a tree. Choosing a partner and settling into marriage was a major life decision and not to be taken lightly. His lifestyle wasn't conducive to marriage. If he hadn't met Daisy, he would have brushed off his mother's comments. Instead, Daisy stood before him front and center in his mind like a song whose lyrics kept running through his head. The effort to forget her grew more difficult every day, every minute.

If she followed through with her plans, she'd be back on the farm with her family in Indiana and enjoying time with her siblings. A smile slowly came over him as he leaned back in the chair at the Internet café and pictured Daisy. He saw her in the barn dressed in jeans and a red flannel shirt, chewing on a long piece of hay.

Mentally kicking himself, he tightened his jaw and his resolve. He was acting like a lovesick teenager; the sensation was new and uncomfortable. If Santa was granting wishes, then he'd put in his request to find a compromise that would bring them together in a way in which neither of them had to give up such a big part of themselves.

Asher missed her far more than he thought was possible. The depth of his feelings didn't make sense. By nature, Asher was practical. Practical and mature. No one would ever think to describe him as impulsive. Yet when it came to Daisy, it felt like his head was in the clouds. Since meeting her, he had become someone he didn't recognize. It seemed impossible that in such a short time span, Daisy had taken over his mind despite his best effort to be rid of her.

He was angry with her.

Angry with himself.

She should never have pushed him.

She should have listened and quietly walked away. He'd told her this was a dead-end romance. She should have believed him. Not Daisy; she'd called him a coward. The insult struck deep and painful. He couldn't forget the proud tilt of her head as she sat in the cab as it drove away.

She hadn't looked back. Not even once.

Later that night, unable to sleep, Asher stared at the ceiling of his quarters while he struggled to chase Daisy from his mind. Every time he closed his eyes she was there, taunting him, claiming he was a weakling.

As if looking to punish himself, he reached for his phone and brought up the one photo he'd taken of her when she was on the Zodiac with a fishing pole in her hand, smiling at him, her eyes bright and alive. A dozen times he'd gone to delete that shot, and each time he found he couldn't make himself do it. It was as if he needed a way to make himself even more depressed.

The only one he could think to talk to was his brother. While Daniel might be ten years older, they were alike in almost every way. Both were logical, rational; both, for the most part, were studious and a little awkward socially. Asher knew his brother was the one who would best understand this situation and advise him.

He hesitated, knowing that the call would likely wake Daniel, but he decided to risk it anyway. His brother picked up on the second ring.

"Asher? I hope you realize what time it is."

"I do."

"Are you okay?"

"For the most part, yes."

"Which tells me you need to talk."

Shuffling noises followed, and Asher suspected his brother was climbing out of bed and finding a spot in the house where they could talk without waking his wife, Kylie. After a few moments, Daniel asked. "Okay, what's up?"

Unsure where to start, Asher asked his brother a question. "Tell me what happened when you met Kylie."

"What? Why are you asking me about that? What's my wife got to do with anything?"

"I need to know how you felt, you know, when you first met her."

"Well," he mumbled, as if rummaging through his memories.

Asher could picture his brother sitting back with his hand braced against his forehead, giving the question consideration.

"I was a resident at the time, working crazy hours at the hospital. I walked into the parking garage and found her name and phone number on my windshield."

"What?" This sounded nothing like the woman Asher knew. "She made a play for you?"

"No, that's not anything Kylie would do. I didn't notice it at the time, but my front headlight on the driver's side was broken. Kylie had pulled out of the parking spot across from me and inadvertently hit my car."

"So that's why she left you her name and phone number."

"Yes. She'd been visiting her father at the hospital and had been upset and wasn't paying attention."

"How is it you never told me this before?"

"Does it matter?"

"No, I suppose not. Go on. You noticed the broken headlight, realized why she'd left her name and number, called her, and the two of you met?"

"I did call, and I thanked her for her honesty. She didn't want to report the accident to her insurance company and said she'd pay for the damage herself."

That was decent of her. "I want to know what you felt when you met her," Asher pressed.

"What do you mean?"

"Were you attracted to her? Did she make you weak in the knees? That sort of thing?"

Daniel made a humming sound, as if reviewing the first meeting with the woman who was to become his wife and the mother of his children. "Not at first, but later."

This conversation wasn't helping the way Asher thought it would. "But you clearly were attracted to her, right?"

"Of course. What guy wouldn't be?"

Still not helpful. "But you saw her again after she paid for the repairs to your car?"

"Yes, I ran into her at the hospital. She was visiting her father again and things weren't going well. She was in tears. I felt badly for her. Because she knew I was a resident heart surgeon, she asked my advice, sort of a second opinion on the best options for her dad. I reviewed her father's chart and then sat with her and her mother and explained that I wouldn't do anything differently than the treatment he was currently receiving. Asher, why all these questions?"

"I've met someone," he said, smiling involuntarily as he said it. Daisy wasn't just someone; she was way above that. The problem was he didn't know what he would or should do about his feelings.

"It's about time. That's great; tell me about her."

"I intend to, but first I need some information from you."

"Sure. Anything."

This was better, and Asher relaxed. "At what point did you realize you and Kylie were meant to be together?"

"At what point?" Daniel said, as if repeating the question aloud would help him find the answer. "Well, I was definitely interested from the first. Not only was Kylie beautiful, I appreciated her honesty. She cared deeply about her father and family, and that appealed to me as well."

"Daisy is close to her family, too."

"Daisy is the name of the woman you seem reluctant to mention?"

"I will talk about her, but first I want to hear about you and Kylie. How soon after you met did you ask her out on a date?"

"A while."

"A while," Asher repeated. Just the way his brother spoke told him there was more to the story than what Daniel was saying. "Can you explain that?"

"If you must know, Kylie had recently gotten out of a yearlong relationship and was gun-shy. When I first asked her out, she refused. I never was much good at this dating business and figured since she turned me down that she wasn't interested."

Asher knew none of this and found it enlightening. His brother had struck out in the beginning with Kylie. At least Daisy had seemed as attracted to him as he was to her, which was encouraging.

"How long was it before you asked her again?"

"I didn't. She contacted me."

"So, she changed her mind?"

"She did, but it was a full year later," Daniel continued. "Kylie sent me a text. Her father had died due to complications with his heart. Following losing her dad, she moved in with her mother, helping Donna ease into widowhood. After a year she moved back into her own apartment. Then one day she saw a car the same model and color as mine, the one she'd backed into, and remembered me. She regretted turning down my dinner invite and reached out. I texted back and we exchanged a few messages over the next couple days. She told me about her dad's passing and asked if I was still interested in meeting for dinner."

"Which you were, obviously."

"More than she would ever have guessed. I'd thought about her a dozen times over that year and wondered if I'd been more persistent if matters would have worked out differently. I kept beating myself up over not trying again."

"How long after that first date did you decide you wanted to marry her?" Asher asked, getting to the point of their conversation.

"Not long. Three months, if that."

"Three months," Asher repeated slowly.

"Okay, three weeks. Make that three days."

Now Asher was smiling. His brother had quickly recognized that Kylie was the one for him. It made Asher wonder if he had let the woman who could be his future walk away. Her parting words rang in his ears like an echo, that he was pushing away the woman who would love him with her whole being. He sucked in a breath, more uncertain now than ever.

"Asher?" Daniel said, pausing in his story. "You okay?"

"I'm good. Please finish about you and Kylie."

"I might have known after three days, but I needed to progress slowly. Kylie'd had two major losses in her life within a short time. I didn't want to overwhelm her by declaring myself too soon. I was patient and managed to hold out for several months."

"All these questions tell me this woman you don't want to talk about is special."

Special didn't start to describe Daisy. "There are complications."

His brother chuckled. "Aren't there always? Is she married? Divorced?"

"Nothing like that."

"Then what's the problem?"

Asher outlined it as best he could, explaining how they'd met and grown close during her convalescence. He was sure to explain why he felt a relationship wouldn't work, detailing their differences.

"You mean to say your Daisy lives here in Chicago?"

"She isn't my Daisy." After everything he'd explained, this was the one fact Daniel wanted to confirm?

"Answer the question."

"Yes, Daisy worked with her partner to establish the online real estate company that has become a household name." Another way to torture himself, Asher had taken to investigating Daisy, Jack Campbell, and the company. What he read confirmed that Daisy was a brilliant executive, hardworking, dedicated, and savvy.

"Is it Easy Home?" Daniel asked.

"That's the one," Asher said.

"Kylie and I used them to find this house."

Asher should have guessed.

"I thought the partnership was with a woman named Everly something or other?"

"Daisy goes by Everly. She changed her name. Said she didn't think anyone in the business world would take a woman named Daisy seriously."

"Asher, this is great news. Does it mean you're considering giving up your vagabond ways and heading into the classroom to teach? I know the university would jump at the chance to hire you."

Daniel was out of his mind. "No."

"No?" his brother repeated. "Why not? You've met the woman, you're—"

"Daisy isn't going to move to Brazil for me," he stated

emphatically. "And I'm not giving up my entire life to be stuffed indoors eight hours a day, so we're at an impasse."

Daniel chuckled. "You're putting up obstacles where there are none, little brother."

Yup, his brother had completely lost his mind. "Come on, Daniel, you know me better than anyone. Can you honestly see me stuck in a classroom? If I'm not outside I become claustrophobic after more than a few hours. Teaching isn't for me any more than living in a big city like Chicago."

If Asher was expecting an argument, Daniel didn't give him one. He had another question.

"Tell me more about her. Let me see her through your eyes."

This wasn't the direction Asher wanted to take. Every mention of Daisy was a pinprick in his chest. "You said it took a year for you and Kylie to reconnect, right?"

"Right. What's that got to do with you and Daisy?"

"Daisy and I hit it off right away. Like gangbusters. I don't know that I've laughed with anyone as much as I did her. The crazy part is this cruise wasn't what she expected." He explained how her loony assistant had arranged it as some sort of revenge.

"You've got to be kidding me."

"I'm not," Asher insisted. "I know it sounds nuts, and at the same time it makes me think I was meant to meet Daisy. After her initial shock, I have to say she was a good sport about it. She was out of her element, but adapted quickly . . .

well, other than a few mishaps along the way, none of which were her fault." He couldn't keep from chuckling as he recalled her misadventures.

"What makes you think she's the one?" Daniel asked.

"I didn't say she's the one," Asher reminded his brother.

"Yes, you did, perhaps not verbally, but your call tells me as much. You're looking at the situation with blinders on, little brother. You sent Daisy on her way and now you can't stop thinking about her. You can't sleep, your mind refuses to forget her. Tell me, when was the last time you felt this strongly about a woman?"

It'd been a mistake to reach out to his brother.

"Asher?" Daniel prompted.

He answered through gritted teeth. "Never."

"That's what I thought."

If Asher could retract this call, he would. "I've only known her two weeks, Daniel. I'd be a fool to give up everything for a woman I've only known for two short weeks."

"Really?"

One word: a probing question.

"Did I hear you mention in your email that the ship is in dock waiting for repairs?"

"Yes, Daisy wanted me to fly to Chicago with her and I refused."

His brother's sigh echoed through Asher's phone. "Seriously?"

"I was saving us the heartache that's sure to follow."

"How's that working for you?"

Yup, it'd been a huge mistake to contact his brother.

"Take the time off, join Kylie and me for Christmas, and while you're here, go see Daisy. You've been apart for a while now. Maybe once you see her, you'll be able to decide what you really want."

Asher wasn't sure about anything any longer. He wasn't keen on leaving Brazil, and yet he was as miserable as he'd ever been. Besides, it wouldn't be easy to get a flight at this late date. "I'll mull it over."

A long, awkward silence followed. "You know what I think?"

It went without saying that Daniel would tell him no matter how he answered.

"It seems to me you need some value clarification," Daniel said. "What is it you really want, Asher? You say you can't breathe in a classroom, and yet isn't that exactly what you're doing on these cruises? You're giving lectures the same way you would in any classroom."

"Yes, but—"

Daniel cut him off. "You claim you need to roam free as you have for the last several years and that's all well and good, but have you noticed, because I certainly have, that you've chosen the least populated areas of the world."

He specialized in both Antarctica and the rainforest. Daniel knew that. Asher opened his mouth to defend himself and then closed it, knowing it would do little good.

"I'm wondering," Daniel continued, "if this is more a case of you protecting your heart."

"Protecting my heart?" Asher protested, thinking the idea ridiculous.

"Think about it, little brother, and get back to me."

CHAPTER FOURTEEN

As promised, a couple days after her arrival, Rose cut and shaped Everly's hair into a bob that was both stylish and flattering. It softened her features; she loved the way her hair framed her face. In more ways than she could count, she felt brand-new.

"You like?" Rose asked, giving her a hand mirror so she could view the back side.

"I love it. Now let me buy you lunch." Her sister had come into the salon on her day off; the least Everly could do was treat Rose at her favorite Mexican restaurant.

"Deal," her sister agreed.

Reaching for their coats, gloves, and scarves, they walked the two blocks down to El Capitan, straining against the wind and the cold. Within minutes they were seated in the restaurant scented with spices, trying to warm themselves once again and holding menus. The threat of snow hung in the air, which put Everly in the mood for soup. When the server appeared, she ordered hot tea and tortilla soup. Rose set aside her menu and ordered spinach enchiladas with sour cream on the side.

"I appreciate the new hairstyle," Everly said, "but you don't need to do this, you know."

"Do what?" Rose frowned and appeared genuinely puzzled.

"Go out of your way to make me . . . I don't know, feel like I belong in this family, I guess."

"What? That's crazy. Of course you belong. All right. I'll admit, it shook all of us last Christmas when you decided to stay in Chicago. We all went through a bit of soul-searching, I think, and realized that business was an excuse." Rose looked down at her hands. "For my part, I thought you felt like you were better than the rest of us."

"Rose, no." Everly felt terrible that her sister would even think such a thing.

"You were always the smart one."

"The nonathletic one."

Rose smiled. "The executive who ruled an empire."

"More like overworked, stressed out, and foolish enough to trust her assistant when she had already proven herself to be a total screwup. And allowed herself to be drawn into Jack's family drama at her expense."

Having heard the story of what Annette had done, Rose merely shook her head. "Dad's favorite," she added.

"Really?" Everly didn't think she was anyone's favorite.

"Until the boys were born," her sister added.

They both laughed and it felt amazingly good. It seemed there'd been misconceptions on both sides. Clearing the air, getting back to being sisters and friends, was what Everly needed most, especially now. Being with Rose gave her strength and helped ease the ache in her heart.

"Did I do anything overtly to make you uncomfortable?" Rose asked.

Everly shrugged. It wasn't what any of her siblings had said or done, it was simply a feeling she'd held for as long as she could remember. "Not really. I'm not like you and Lily and the twins . . . oh, those boys, don't get me started."

Rose cocked her eyebrows and nodded. "Yup, those two are something else. You are different than Lily and me, I suppose, but that doesn't make you any less important or any less loved."

"I can't do half the things you and Lily do. I'm not athletic. Remember what my first sewing project looked like? And—"

"Stop." Rose flattened her hand on the tabletop. "You were never meant to play soccer or sit behind a sewing machine. That isn't you. It doesn't make you any less or any better. We all have our talents, Daisy. Yours just happen to be different from the ones Lily and I have. You went after your dream and Lily and I did, too. Because those dreams didn't match yours doesn't make any one of us less than the other."

"Why is everyone going out of their way like this? It's disconcerting." All the fuss made her uneasy.

"Daisy, don't you know? We've missed you. Last Christmas was the worst. It felt as if a deep, dark hole had developed in our family. Even caroling and the hayride felt off without you there."

"I should have been here." Everly regretted that now.

"Yes, you should have. I think each one of us decided to do whatever it took to make sure you didn't want to stay away for Christmas ever again."

"None of this is necessary, I learned my lesson. I'm happy to be home for Christmas. If nothing else, the cruise taught me to appreciate what I have."

Rose reached for her napkin, removed the paper band, and released her silverware. "I'm glad you brought that up. You want to tell me, sister to sister, what happened on the cruise?"

Everly reached for her own silverware. "Not really." She hadn't stopped thinking about Asher from the moment she'd left Brazil. He was the one who'd insisted it had to end then and there. If she were to move forward, she had to put him out of her mind . . . not that it was working. He was constantly in her thoughts, despite her best efforts to put him behind her and look toward the future.

"It might help," Rose urged gently.

"His name's Asher, the naturalist aboard the Amazon Explorer, and I was foolish enough to fall for him," she said, her voice low to hide her heartache. "Unfortunately, the feelings were more one-sided than I thought." It embarrassed her to think of how she'd laid her heart before him only to have him stomp all over it.

As if reading the pain in her sister's eyes, Rose leaned forward and placed her hand over Everly's.

"I don't have any option but to accept that he didn't feel as strongly about me as I do him. To Asher, I was nothing more than a shipboard romance. He claims otherwise. But what else am I to think when he let me walk away?"

Rose's face tightened. "Then he doesn't deserve you."

Everly knew that wasn't the case. Unwilling to argue, she played along. Nodding, she said, "You're absolutely right. I'm moving on."

"Good for you."

It was better to put all that behind her, or so she kept telling herself. "But it hurts," she added in a whisper.

"Of course it does." Her sister's eyes filled with sympathy.

Everly was grateful when their meals were served, as she didn't want to discuss Asher any longer.

Rose dug into the enchiladas with vigor. "I skipped breakfast . . . I know, I know, bad idea. With all the Christmas goodies around and my low resistance level, I'm trying to avoid gaining weight. Don't ask how well this is working, and spare me the embarrassment of lying. I envy you. You weigh the same as you did in high school, don't you?"

"No, I'm a few pounds heavier."

"Yeah, right," Rose said, glaring at her. "If you weren't my little sister and brilliant to boot, I could hate you."

"I wasn't so brilliant in Brazil," Everly said, mentally recalling her misadventures. She might be at the top of her game when it came to orchestrating a business transaction, but when she ventured into the unspoiled beauty of the Brazilian rainforest, she'd been lost in more ways than one. Forging through the jungle in what can only be described as a monsoon wasn't her idea of fun. Only it had been. Asher had made it so, leaving her with memories that would last a lifetime.

Her sister was eager to hear about her cruise, and under normal circumstances Everly would have been happy to relay her many escapades. However, any mention of her trip would include Asher, the one person she was determined to put out of her mind.

Halfway through her meal, Everly's phone pinged and she noticed it was a message from Jack. She ignored it and set it back inside her purse. Everly was all too aware that Jack would use whatever he felt was necessary to get her back inside the office, having conveniently forgotten his impromptu offer of a month off.

Rose studied her. "Do you need to get that?" she asked.

"Nope."

"It wasn't work, then?"

"It was, only I'm choosing to ignore it." Jack could learn, the same way she had, to handle whatever crisis floated across his desk. It was baptism by fire. Everly had no doubt he'd come through just fine. Jack was fully capable. For years he'd become accustomed to having Everly deal with anything the least bit demanding. And she'd let him.

Well, no longer.

Everly had been foolish to think she was the only problem-solver in the company.

Rose looked stunned. "It could be important."

Everly nodded. "It probably is. When Jack won't be able to reach me, he'll need to figure it out himself without relying on me. And that will be good for him." Good for them both.

Feeling slightly guilty to be ignoring Jack, she sent him a quick text, claiming that whatever the issue was he could handle it and wishing him the best. They were partners, after all. It was well past time for Jack to carry his share of the weight.

"What's this I hear about you wanting to build a gingerbread house with all the kids?" Rose asked after she pushed her clean plate aside. "Talk about swimming with the sharks."

Everly smiled to herself. Her sister knew nothing about her tumble into piranha-infested waters. If she survived that, a gingerbread house with a few rambunctious kids was nothing.

They finished their meal, Everly paid, and they started walking back to the salon.

School would be out for the holidays soon and the gingerbread house was a family tradition. Their mother invited all the grandchildren old enough to participate to gather at the farm. Seeing that Everly was home, she decided to join in on the fun.

Most of the work would be done by their mother, but Everly was all in. She'd bought a small fortune in candy from the local candy store, the very one where she'd spent a good portion of her allowance as a child, to decorate the gingerbread house.

The plan was for Mom to bake the gingerbread into the shape of a cottage. Later that afternoon Everly and her mother would glue it together with frosting. They'd decided to give it overnight to harden so that little fingers wouldn't demolish it.

"You know Mom. Any opportunity she has to pass along family traditions and she's gung-ho," Everly reminded her sister.

"Yes, but it's Mom's thing," Rose said. "What made you decide to help? It's going to be messy and the kids will eat far more candy than will ever end up on Candy Cane Lane."

What her sister said was true, but Everly didn't mind. "It'll be fun. It always is, and I have to make up for the time I squandered last Christmas."

Rose shook her head and rolled her eyes. "You have no idea of what you're getting yourself into, little sister."

Rose was right. The following afternoon, Everly's sisters' children eagerly gathered around the kitchen table. The bare gingerbread house sat in the middle of an aluminum foil–covered piece of cardboard. Little ones jockeyed for space to paste pieces of candy to the roof and sides. They licked their fingers in between, smearing frosting over their faces. Dealing with a thousand brokers was easier than supervising her nieces and nephews, high on sugar and excitement. Everly loved it, laughing with them and her mother. This was Christmas and the very traditions she had once loved.

By the time they were finished, the gingerbread house was covered in red licorice, peanut M&M's, Skittles, and Tootsie Rolls, plus a dozen other small candies. Part of the roof decorations disappeared as quickly as they were pressed into place. While Everly's patience had been stretched to the max, she'd never laughed more in her life, certainly not in the last several years.

Except when she'd been with Asher. The thought flooded her brain before she dismissed it and him.

When the children finished, they proudly showed the house to their grandfather. Before they left, Everly's nieces and nephews had all hugged her, smearing candy juices on her blouse.

When the last one was out the door, Everly, exhausted but giddy, flopped down onto a kitchen chair. Her mother brought her a warm cup of homemade eggnog. "Here, we could both use this."

Everly gratefully accepted the glass. "I hope you spiked this with a liberal dose of rum."

Her mother responded with a confirming smile. "We've earned it." Her eyes glistened with tears. "It's so good to have you home this year, Daisy."

She was back.

Finding her way back to the woman she had once been.

Back to where she understood the importance of family. Of traditions. Of celebration.

Back to enjoying Christmas.

Asher's immediate reaction to his brother's statement was a flat denial. Yes, he'd had a couple relationships go south. He was willing to admit that both had been painful. He'd managed to come out the other side without scar tissue, or so he believed.

Something else he was willing to admit: His time with

Daisy was unique. The guests who booked the Antarctica and Amazon adventures were almost always retired couples. It was rare to host single young women. Not only had Daisy arrived unaccompanied, he'd spent far and away more alone time with her than he had with any other guest.

Almost from the first day, he'd been smitten with her. Who wouldn't? She was gorgeous, funny, smart, savvy, and far out of his league. That didn't stop him while she was on board, but he was smart enough to know this relationship was doomed to fail. He'd done his best to protect his heart, made sure she understood that there was no hope of a future together, and let her go. It was the smart thing to do for them both.

That was the game plan. He sent her off, convinced that once she was out of sight, he would forget her.

To admit his plan had backfired would be an understatement.

Daisy was constantly on his mind. He tried to fight it, wondered if there might be a possibility of making something real and lasting out of this attraction. For that reason alone, he'd contacted his brother. What he hadn't expected was for Daniel to gut-punch him with questions he didn't want to answer.

After a day filled with denial, grumbling under his breath, refuting Daniel's claims, Asher was having second thoughts. First and foremost, Asher didn't need his values or his priorities clarified. If anyone was aware of his strengths and weaknesses, it was him.

One point he was willing to concede was the fact that his lectures were akin to what he would do as a professor. He remembered his own classes and the enjoyment he'd gotten from both learning about nature and exploring a variety of areas around the world to complete his studies. Teaching at the university level, he would be able to do both as he once had as a student. It boggled his mind that he hadn't considered this earlier.

Another day passed and Asher was reluctantly willing to consider the second part of the conversation he'd had with his brother. By cutting off any contact with Daisy, he had been protecting his own heart. It would be wonderful if there was a way for them to be together long-term, but he couldn't see that happening. Then why, he asked himself, had he been unable to stop thinking about her? She was on his mind constantly. It didn't help that he found himself staring at the photo he took of her ten or more times a day.

Unable to sleep, he pulled up his phone and stared at Daisy's face again. His heart ached.

He hit the call button and waited for Daniel to answer.

"Why is it you can't manage to call me at any other time than the middle of the night?" Daniel muttered, sounding none too pleased to be hearing from him.

"Okay, you win."

"Is there a prize?" Daniel asked on the tail end of a yawn.

"Very funny. I'm booking a flight to Chicago. As soon as I have the details, I'll text you."

Asher expected some show of pleasure, but none followed. "Did you hear what I said?"

"I did. Just need to know who you're coming to see? Me or Daisy?"

Asher growled under his breath. "If you must know, both."

"Good. That's what I wanted to hear."

CHAPTER FIFTEEN

"Dinner!" her mother shouted up the stairwell.

Everly sat on top of her bed, staring at the computer screen after answering emails from the team regarding Jack's handling of the latest crisis. She was pleased. As she knew he would, he'd managed a difficult real estate developer who had threatened to pull out of a deal. Crisis averted. Everly knew Jack felt good about it. She was relieved that her faith in her partner hadn't been misplaced.

Hearing her mother's voice, Everly bounced off the bed and bounded down the stairs. With Christmas the following week, she'd been busy every minute with family and church events. Her sisters had made the effort to make sure she felt included, and Everly had done her own part. It felt good to be home. There was no place else she'd rather be to nurse her tender heart. Her mother hadn't pried. Rose was the only one she'd told about Asher. It needed to be that way. Everly needed her family, not their sympathy.

On Friday she'd attended the school program for her nieces and nephews, followed by cookies and lemonade afterward. Russell and Lily's two boys, Denny and Scottie, had proudly introduced her to their teachers.

Saturday morning, Everly volunteered with members of the community church to deliver food baskets to families in need. Sunday morning, following the church service, her father gave the kids from the congregation sleigh rides while Everly and her two sisters helped their mother serve hot apple cider to those awaiting a turn on the sleigh.

Monday morning, the receptionist at the hair salon where Rose worked called in sick at the last minute, so Everly had filled in for the day. She got a free pedicure for her effort, although she would have willingly paid for it.

"I'll set the table," Everly said, coming into the kitchen. "How many for dinner tonight?" she asked, pulling open the silverware drawer, ready to count out the forks and knives.

"Just the three of us," her mother said.

That was a switch. Every night since her return, company had shown up for dinner. Her siblings, their families, aunts, uncles, and assorted cousins had made their way to the farm. No one needed an invitation, or an excuse. There was always enough.

Although her parents had an empty nest, it seemed like her mother was unable to cook a meal for fewer than seven. It had become a family joke, yet nothing ever seemed to go to waste.

"Jeff said he might stop by after dinner," her father shouted from the living room.

"Good."

Her brother was sure to take home any leftovers, and probably enough to feed him and his family for two or three dinners.

While the reconnecting with her two sisters had gone well, it hadn't been the same with her twin brothers. Jeff and John had a beef with her skipping out on Christmas the year before and weren't inclined to keep their opinions to themselves.

"Guess we should count our blessings that you decided to grace us with your presence this year," John had said when he first saw her. His hug was long and hard, as if he feared she might try to escape again.

"What's that supposed to mean?" Everly asked, although she knew.

"It means we're happy you're here this Christmas," Jeff had added.

Yup, it did seem her brothers had gotten the message. "Staying in Chicago was a mistake I don't intend to repeat."

Jeff and John smiled. "Glad to hear it," they'd said in unison. Even now it was difficult to tell the two apart. They personified the term identical twins.

"I plan on sticking around for a while after Christmas, too," she'd told them.

The two shared a look. "Did you have a falling-out with Campbell?" John asked.

"Nope."

Jeff chuckled and elbowed his brother. "No way, Jack's too smart to let anything like that happen."

Everly laughed; her brothers weren't far from wrong.

"What's for dinner?" her father asked, wandering into the kitchen and breaking into her thoughts.

"Meat loaf," her mother answered, bent in half, her backside sticking out as she pulled the pan out of the oven. "With scalloped potatoes."

"Green beans?"

"Yup, and salad. Do I have your approval?"

Everly's dad kissed his wife's cheek while wrapping his arms around her waist. "That's my favorite dinner, as well you know."

Everly smiled, enjoying the exchange between her parents. She knew there'd been times when they'd disagreed, but she would never doubt their love for each other. It was that kind of partnership she'd hoped to find one day herself. Only it wouldn't be with Asher.

"Didn't you say last night's dinner was your favorite?" Everly teased her dad.

"Every meal your mother makes is my favorite," he returned.

Following dinner and dishes, Everly sat down at the piano and played several classic Christmas songs until Jeff arrived. He brought along his wife, Marlene, and his three-month-old son, Andrew. Everly had little experience when it came to infants. When Marlene asked her if she wanted to hold the baby, Everly hesitated and then decided she should.

Marlene carefully handed Everly the sleeping babe. Nestled in her embrace, Andrew's tiny mouth formed little milk bubbles. She gazed down at him, content and at peace. For his part, little Andrew looked as if this was exactly where he wanted to be. After a moment, he opened his eyes, looked up at her, cooed, and smiled. Everly smiled back and tickled him beneath his chin.

"You might make a good mother after all," Jeff teased.

"Thanks, Jeff." To her surprise, she found the thought of motherhood didn't terrify her.

"You'll make a wonderful mother," her mother countered automatically, as if this was never in question. "When you were little you used to play endlessly with your dolls."

"I did?" Everly didn't remember that. "I must have been really young."

"You doted on your brothers, too."

"Their crying bothered me." She recalled fighting with Rose and Lily for a chance to hold one of the twins when they first came home from the hospital. She'd been little herself and hadn't been allowed to. As she remembered, she'd pouted and thrown an epic temper tantrum.

Her brother and his family had stayed for an hour when Everly reluctantly released the baby to her sister-in-law. She was about to head up to bed when she got an urgent text message from Jack. He'd routinely reached out a few times each day with a question or two he needed help answering.

Everly hadn't completely ignored his panicked pleas for help. She wouldn't do that to Jack. He needed reassurance and she gave it to him. She listened but didn't offer advice, rather letting him sort out how he intended to handle the situation. Only once had she advised a different tactic. Jack was more capable than he realized.

She responded right away to his current text. No sooner had she hit the send button when her phone rang. It was Jack.

"Merry Christmas," she greeted.

"It's not so merry around here," he grumbled. "Do you realize how late it is? I'm still at the office."

Everly noticed it was well past seven. She'd spent far too many nights working late; it was fitting justice that Jack put in his share of overtime. This was probably the latest Jack had stayed at the office in the last six years.

"I should be home with my family," he complained.

Everly didn't remind him of her own late nights, but he got it. Jack knew, and that alone was better than anything she could have said.

"Jack, you're doing great."

"Nice of you to say so," he muttered, even more disgruntled.

"I'm proud of you," she added, and she sincerely meant it. "You handled the situation with the Stone Developers better than I would have."

"Don't joke, Everly."

"I'm not joking. I said as much in my email."

"Another problem has popped up," he said disgustedly. "What's with these people? Don't they realize it's almost Christmas?"

"Tell me about it."

Jack took ten minutes to relay the details. Everly listened but didn't offer advice. Jack was in charge. "What do you intend to do about it?" she asked.

"What would you do?"

"I'm not the one at the office, Jack. You are."

His every word was loaded with reluctance as he gave her the particulars of how he intended to resolve the issue. She found herself nodding at each point.

"That's exactly what I would do."

Jack huffed out a satisfied sigh. "Good."

"Is there anything else?" she asked.

"There's something I need to ask you," he said, and she sensed the same reluctance that she had earlier.

"Fire away."

Jack hesitated before he spoke. "It didn't take me long to

realize my mistake in insisting you stay away from the office. It was stupid on my part, an effort to keep the peace between me, my mother, and my sister. I made a mistake ever agreeing to let Annette come work for the firm, and it's cost me dearly."

Everly appreciated that he recognized this.

"The thing is, Everly, I have this gut feeling you aren't going to come back." He hesitated, and it sounded like he was holding his breath before plunging ahead with his question. "Are you? Will you be back come January?"

CHAPTER SIXTEEN

Everly hadn't really answered Jack's question. Until he'd asked if she was going to return to Easy Home, she hadn't considered that as an option. As soon as he posed the possibility, it struck her that selling her half of the company had been playing in the back of her mind since her return. Now that he'd voiced it, she'd begun considering it without addressing it openly.

Jack hadn't pressured her for an answer; although he'd been quick to explain how badly the company needed her. He continued by saying it would devastate him and the entire team if she were to choose to leave. He added several inducements about taking on a larger part of the responsibilities and made promises Everly wasn't sure he could or would keep. For the first few weeks, she knew Jack would put in the effort and then gradually everything would return to the way it was before she left for the cruise.

"Was that Jack again?" her mother asked, once Everly was off the phone.

"Isn't it always?" she joked. The only other calls she'd received had been from her friend Lizzy and her two sisters. Everly felt a wave of peace at the realization that she got along better with Rose and Lily now than she had at any other time. It was enlightening that while they might have different skills and interests, they were a lot alike, too.

After that initial talk at the Mexican restaurant, Rose hadn't asked Everly about Asher again. She was grateful her sister had kept her confidence. Her heart hurt, but each day she was away from the Amazon and Asher, the ache dulled a little more. Before long he would be nothing more than a distant memory.

That's what she told herself. And if she said it often enough, she might even start to believe it.

"Is anything wrong?" her mother asked. "You looked so serious when you hung up. Jack isn't demanding you return to Chicago, is he?"

"Not at all." Everly sat down at the kitchen table and her mother joined her. "He asked me if I intended on ever coming back." The shock of the question continued to rattle her. Deep down he must have sensed that this matter was weighing on her mind as well as on his.

Her mother's eyes widened with surprise. "Are you?"

"I . . . I don't know. After the cruise I made it clear to Jack that changes needed to be made. He listened, but I'm not convinced he heard me. Then again, maybe he did and that's what prompted him to ask."

"You're considering it. I can tell by the look in your eyes."

Her mother had a succinct way of looking at problems. What her mother didn't know was that Everly had been weighing the direction of her future before this conversation with Jack.

She squeezed Everly's hand. "Your heart will guide you, and when it does, you'll know the right answer." Lois Lancaster stood long enough to pour them each a cup of coffee and bring out what was left of Grandma Ruth's fudge.

Everly reached for the coffee mug and took a piece of fudge. "Grandma's fudge always makes things better," she joked.

"It sure does."

Climbing the stairs sometime later, Everly's head felt full, her thoughts buzzing like a swarm of bees searching for a place to settle. Her mother had suggested she listen to her heart. Everly had done that with Asher, convinced she was as important to him as he was to her. She'd been wrong. Dead wrong. She'd been so sure, confident, and she'd been misled by her own heart.

As she undressed for bed, she paused with one leg out of

her jeans. Selling out wasn't a decision to be made impul-
sively. If she were to leave the company, she didn't have a
single idea of what she would do with herself afterward. She
would need to secure her future. Real estate wasn't an option, as she had signed a noncompete clause. It would need
to be something new and fresh, something she would enjoy,
and, if possible, something that would give her the time she
needed to find herself again.

The idea of traveling appealed to her, but it wouldn't be
nearly as much fun alone. She remembered the Browns and
the adventures they'd shared as they'd explored the world together. Never one to sit idle, Everly knew she'd soon grow
restless and bored without a game plan. The change from
working sixty hours a week to none would be way too drastic. Naturally, the transition would take time. She'd never
leave the company if she didn't believe it would continue on
the same successful path without her.

Her mother had made sure Everly knew she was welcome
to move home, should she decide to sell. She could live with
her parents until she decided what she wanted to do next. It
was a generous offer, but not one Everly would consider.

Did she want to sell her half of Easy Home?

That remained the question.

It shook Everly that she didn't have the answer.

A month ago, if anyone had asked her, she would have
unequivocally refused to consider giving up the company she
and Jack had built from the ground up. The mere thought

would've caused her to break into peals of laughter at the outrageous idea.

It didn't sound nearly as ludicrous now, though.

While Jack insisted the company needed her, that without her leadership, he would stumble, he wouldn't. It would be a big adjustment, but all would be well.

As Everly lay in bed, staring up at the dark ceiling, she wanted to blame Asher for this indecision. His rejection had badly shaken her, to the point that she questioned everything—where she belonged and what was right for her moving forward.

Rolling onto her side and tucking the warm blanket around her shoulders, Everly decided to give herself time. She'd mull over her options after Christmas.

Asher was dog tired. He'd taken a red-eye flight from Brazil and landed at O'Hare when most people were answering the call of their alarm clock. His brother picked him up at the airport and dropped him off at the house before heading to the hospital.

For a good part of the flight, Asher had been wide awake. His thoughts were heavy. He had to be back to the Amazon Explorer the day after Christmas. He'd already wasted an entire week, which gave him only seven days to patch things up with Daisy . . . if she'd let him.

Even now, he couldn't forget the look in her eyes when he

made it plain he wasn't interested in continuing their relationship. Fool. Fool. Fool. Daisy had flinched as if she'd taken a blow. For a few awkward seconds she'd said nothing before nodding and accepting his decision, although he could see it devastated her. Without an argument, she'd climbed into the cab and headed straight to the airport.

Exhausted from the flight, Asher slept for a good portion of the day. That evening he joined his brother for dinner with the family. The house was beautifully decorated for Christmas. The tree was in the main living area off the kitchen; it had a variety of homemade ornaments the children had crafted. Another tree was placed in the living room, decorated with a creative flair that would make a designer proud. Several Nativity sets were scattered about the house.

Asher envied Daniel his marriage. He'd found his soul mate and they'd created a great life together. Come morning, Asher would drive to Indiana and, he hoped, connect with Daisy. He wasn't sure of his welcome. Wasn't sure Daisy would be willing to give him a third chance. He could hope, but until they met face-to-face, the unknown hung over his head like a dark rain cloud.

"Asher," Kylie said, distracting him from his musings. "Is something wrong with dinner? You've barely touched your food. If it isn't to your liking, I can fix you something else."

Asher forced a smile. "No, no, there's nothing wrong. Dinner is lovely. The problem is mine."

Daniel and Kylie exchanged looks. They seemed to be able to communicate without speaking, which amazed him. He wondered if that would have been the case between him and Daisy one day.

"How about a drink?" Daniel suggested after the dinner dishes had been cleared away. "I have a bottle of single-barrel Scotch I've been meaning to open."

A wee dram of Scotch sounded ideal, exactly what Asher needed. Seeing that he'd spent several hours sleeping, he wasn't sure how well he'd manage that night.

His brother led him into the den and pushed a button that started the gas fireplace and then excused himself. "Give me a few minutes. I'm reading Dickens's A Christmas Carol to the kids and they're anxious to hear the next chapter. We're at the part where the first of the three ghosts appears."

"Take all the time you need."

After a while, the French doors to the den opened and Daniel came into the room. "Sorry, that took longer than I thought it would."

Asher was surprised to realize that his brother had been away nearly forty minutes. Buried deep in his thoughts, mulling over all the might-have-beens, he hadn't noticed the passage of time. For all the attention he'd paid, Daniel could have been gone five minutes.

Kylie followed behind with the bottle of Scotch and two glasses.

Daniel kissed his wife, wrapping his arms around her trim waist, and whispered in her ear something Asher couldn't hear. The affection between the two struck a raw nerve, and he was forced to look away.

"We won't be long," Daniel assured his wife, taking hold of her hand as she started to leave.

"Take your time, I've got gifts to wrap and cookies to bake."

Kylie left and closed the French doors. Daniel moved behind his massive desk, opened the bottle of Scotch, and poured them each a couple inches before handing a glass to Asher.

They sat in the two leather chairs that faced the fireplace. Asher breathed in the aroma of the Scotch and swore it curled his nose hairs. This was mighty fine Scotch. The best. He was honored his brother chose to share it with him.

Asher took his first sip, closed his eyes, and savored the liquor. For a long moment, he stared into the flickering flames in the fireplace, reviewing what he would say to Daisy when he saw her again.

"I'm driving to Indiana tomorrow," he told his brother.

"Figured as much."

Asher stared down at the amber liquid as the doubts beat against the thick wall of his pride. "I'm nervous."

"I can't say I blame you."

Asher held on to the Scotch glass with both hands. "I've

badly bungled this relationship. I don't know if Daisy will even talk to me, and frankly, if she doesn't, I won't blame her."

Daniel crossed his legs and leaned back against the leather wing chair. "What if she turns you away?"

Asher looked up and frowned. He'd expected words of encouragement and support from his brother. He had enough doubts of his own without his brother reminding him of what a fool he'd been.

"Do you have a plan B?" Daniel asked.

Asher didn't. Not really.

"A more important question, Ash: What if Daisy is over-joyed to see you?"

That was his hope.

"Then what?" Daniel pressed. "Do you plan to kiss her, wish her a Merry Christmas, and then head back to Brazil?"

The question shook him. At this point, all he knew was that he needed to see Daisy again; what happened after that was as clear as the murky waters of the Amazon River. His brother was right, though. Other than his heart, none of the circumstances that kept them apart had changed.

"From the blank look you're giving me, I'd say you haven't thought that far ahead."

Asher felt foolish. What was he thinking?

"Are you going to ask her to leave her job and join you in Brazil? If you do that, then you'll see each other for, what . . .

an hour or two every couple weeks when you return before you start the next cruise?"

"No." He'd never ask that of Daisy. But where would that leave him? The seriousness of this question pressed heavy against his shoulders.

Daniel wasn't finished. "Are you willing to move to Chicago in order to be with her?"

That was the very question Asher hadn't wanted to ask himself. Now it was front and center and required an answer. One of them would need to make a change, and the logical choice was him. Setting aside his Scotch, Asher leaned forward and braced his elbows against his knees while he ran his hands through his hair. He remembered Daisy telling him compromises would need to be made and questions would need to be answered. The first of those questions was how much of himself was he willing to give to make this relationship work?

He could see that his brother was patiently waiting for his response. "That is the big question, isn't it?"

"Seems to me it is," Daniel agreed. "Do you have an answer?"

Did he? Asher weighed his options. He loved Daisy. It'd taken him long enough to admit his feelings. To uproot his entire life for love seemed drastic and unreasonable. Could he do it? Should he?

"Asher?" his brother prodded.

"I could teach."

"That's always been an option. The university would welcome you. The question is if that is what you want."

Asher straightened and the truth came to him. "Yes, if it means I can have Daisy in my life." It was then that he knew. Whatever Daisy decided, he would give his notice to the Explorer cruise lines. His "vagabond days" were over. They had served their purpose, given him the life experience he'd craved. The time had come to move on and share his love and passion with students who would go out into the world and make a difference the way he'd always sought to do.

Daniel grinned as if he'd known what Asher would decide all along. "Good luck tomorrow, little brother."

Asher had the strongest feeling that he was going to need it.

CHAPTER SEVENTEEN

Everly woke to sunshine beaming in the bedroom window. The clock showed it was after eight. In farm country, that was midmorning. Tossing aside the covers, she leaped out of bed and dressed in jeans, a thick sweater, and boots before bounding down the stairs feeling guilty for being so lazy.

Her mother was busy in the laundry room off the kitchen, sorting the wash, when Everly burst into the room.

"Mom," she said, "you should have woken me."

"Why? My guess is you had a lot on your mind when you went to bed. How are you feeling this morning?"

"Better," Everly said. "It took me until after three to fall asleep."

"Did you make a decision?"

Everly had to think about it. "Not really. I figure I'll put it on the back burner until we get through the holidays. This isn't something I want to decide on the spur of the moment. If I do sell, I'll want a have a plan for what's next."

Her mother nodded and then went back to sorting clothes. "You know your father and I will support you, regardless."

"Thanks, Mom," she said and then asked, "What can I do to help?"

"I was thinking of making a big pot of spaghetti for dinner. Would you mind getting the meat out of the freezer and bringing me up a couple jars of canned tomatoes?"

"I'm on it." Everly raced down the stairs to the cellar where the family stored the jars of home-canned produce that came from the large garden her mother kept every summer. Some of Everly's favorite memories revolved around the garden. Eating fresh strawberries warm from the sun, the red juice running down her chin. Shelling peas with her two sisters on the front porch swing and snapping green beans.

Her mother's recipe called for the sauce to simmer on the stove all day. When she was a kid, it had been one of her favorite dinners. Her mother knew that and was cooking this meal especially for her.

As she came up the stairs, she heard Jasper barking. Glancing out the window, Everly noticed a strange car parked in the yard.

"Are you expecting anyone?" she called out to her mother.

"Not me, but your father might. He's got a couple heads of beef he's looking to sell."

Turning away from the window, Everly set the frozen hamburger and canned jars of tomatoes on the kitchen counter. Knowing the spices her mother used, she reached into the cupboard and brought down the basil, oregano, thyme, and granulated garlic.

"I'm going back upstairs to comb my hair," she called to her mother just as the back door opened, letting in Jasper, her father, and Asher Adams.

Everly froze, unable to move.

"I take it you know this young man," her father said, directing the question to her.

Her voice had completely deserted her.

"Daisy?"

"I know him," she answered, after an awkward silence.

Her mother came out of the laundry room and looked from Everly to Asher and then back again. "Is this the guy you didn't want to talk about?" she asked in a stage whisper.

Everly nodded.

"My name's Asher Adams," he said, stepping forward and extending his hand to her mother.

"Why are you here?" Everly asked. She was too shocked to think clearly and realized her question lacked warmth and welcome.

"I heard you mention something about fudge. I have a weakness for it. Grandma Ruth's recipe, I believe you said."

"You came to talk to me about fudge?"

"Daisy," her mother gently chastised. "Asher is our guest. Why don't you invite him into the living room?"

All she seemed capable of doing was staring at him as if he was an alien from outer space.

"I'm sure after the long drive you'd welcome a cup of coffee," her mother offered, seeing Everly's complete lack of manners.

"I'd like that," Asher said, although his eyes didn't waver from Daisy.

Her father led him into the other room and Jasper followed.

"Daisy, my goodness, what's the matter with you?" her mother asked in a low whisper. "Your young man is here. Talk to him."

"My hair isn't combed. I don't have any makeup on." Leave it to Asher to show up when she looked her worst. It surprised her he didn't take one look at her and run for the hills.

"From the way he's looking at you, I don't think he much cares."

"I care," she insisted.

Her mother thrust the coffee mug into her hands and steered her toward the other room.

Everly jolted forward and nearly spilled the hot liquid. Taking short, tentative steps, she walked into the living room as if heading toward the guillotine.

"Gary," her mother said, following close behind her. "Let's give these young people a chance to talk in private."

Everly sat across from Asher, her flattened hands tucked between her knees, her eyes downcast, waiting. Neither spoke for several uneasy moments.

"I've missed you," Asher said.

"Then it wasn't the fudge that convinced you to fly from Brazil after all?"

Asher grinned and shook his head. "I was a fool to let you go, Daisy. I've regretted it every minute since you left. I thought within a day or two I'd be able to move on."

"How did that work for you?" she asked, although his being here was answer enough.

He snickered softly. "Not well at all. You were all I could think about, all I wanted to think about." He glanced up then. "Do I dare hope you thought of me?"

She shrugged. "Not really."

His lips quivered as if he was holding back a laugh. "You're a terrible liar."

"Okay, if you must know, you crossed my mind every now and again."

He cocked his eyebrow in skepticism, but he didn't pursue the question further. "Before you left you told me there would be obstacles we'd need to face, questions we'd need to answer, and compromises to make."

She nodded. "I remember."

"You said you were willing, and hoped that I would be, too."

She held her breath. "Are you . . . willing?"

Instead of answering, Asher stood and walked over to the fireplace, where the family stockings hung. He stared at the one with her name on it before he turned to face her. "My brother asked me if I was willing to move to Chicago."

"You hate the city."

"I told him I would if it meant I could be with you."

Everly scooted to the edge of the cushion. "Do you mean it?"

"With all my heart."

Everly stood and walked directly into his arms. When he brought her into his embrace, a sigh went through her as she clung to him. His mouth sought hers in a kiss that was hot enough to ignite fireworks. It felt right and good to have Asher's arms around her.

They couldn't seem to get enough of each other. Kissing again and again, whispering to each other of the loneliness and the regrets. "I missed you every minute of every day," she admitted between kisses when she could find her breath.

"Knew it," Asher whispered, his voice husky and warm, as if he was alive again now that she was in his embrace.

Everly jabbed Asher in his ribs with her index finger. He grinned and braced his forehead against hers. "I've had a lot of sleepless nights."

"Me, too," she admitted. "I . . . I don't know if I'm going back to Easy Home."

Asher took a step away, as if uncertain he'd heard her correctly. "Don't, Daisy, not for me. I'll take a position at the college and we can go from there. See where this takes us."

"Selling out has been on my mind for a while now, only I hadn't realized until Jack voiced it. I'm giving it serious consideration."

She was about to say more when Rose burst into the living room like an avenging angel, followed close behind by Lily.

Hands on her hips, glaring at Asher, Rose said, with her eyes full of fire, "You don't deserve my sister."

Asher grinned down at Everly. "Can't say I have much of an argument there."

"Rose, please," Everly said, waving her arms at her sister.

"You broke Daisy's heart," Lily said, equally irate. She, too, braced her hands against her hips and then looked to Daisy and lowered her voice. "Rose told me, but only because I made her."

Almost immediately, her brothers Jeff and John stormed into the room.

"Is this the guy?" Jeff asked Rose, nodding in Asher's direction.

It seemed it wasn't only Lily she'd told, but both her brothers as well.

"Will all of you hold your horses. Asher is here because

he . . . because he wants us to come to an understanding." He hadn't declared his feelings other than to say he wanted to be wherever she was.

"I'll make him understand," John threatened, growling out the words.

"We both will."

"Get a rope," Jeff said.

Everly burst out laughing. She couldn't help it. Looping her arms around Asher's neck, she kissed him so that her siblings would never doubt her feelings. Asher grabbed hold of her head, weaving his fingers into her hair and angling her mouth over his. When they broke apart, the room had gone quiet.

"You'll have to forgive my family," she said, loud enough for everyone to hear. "They're a little overprotective."

"Are you willing to take him back?" Jeff asked.

Everly smiled up at Asher. "I'm thinking about it."

"Don't think too long," Asher said. "Your brothers look like they'd welcome the opportunity to take me down."

"The things a woman has to do for her man," Everly said, her eyes smiling.

"He's not taking you back to Brazil." This was a firm statement by Rose.

"Not on the agenda," Asher assured them.

"Good thing," Jeff and John said in stereo.

"A very good thing," Everly added, her arm around Asher and his around her.

"Seems our work here is done," Rose said, and ushered her siblings out of the room.

The days leading up to Christmas were everything Everly hoped they would be. Asher stayed with her family for two days. Everly made sure they made the most of their brief time together. He agreed to go Christmas shopping with her for her nieces and nephews. He advised her and she advised him about gifts for his own family.

After they had made their purchases, they had pizza for lunch. Everly was ready to head back to the farm, but Asher had one last stop he wanted to make.

A jewelry store.

"I saw this earlier," he said, pointing out an intricate gold necklace. "It reminded me of you. Delicate yet strong. Beautiful and bright."

It was the most stunning piece of goldwork Everly had ever seen. "Asher, it's too much."

"Not for you and the way I feel about you. I won't be here for Christmas, so let me give it to you now."

Everly thought her heart would burst. She'd never owned anything of this quality. After he made the purchase, Asher stood behind her and placed it around her neck.

"Thank you," she whispered nearly choking on the emotion as she fingered it.

———

Both evenings they played cards with her parents and whoever else showed, usually one of her brothers. Asher proved to be a good player, although she was convinced he cheated. He ate every piece of fudge and candy she put before him, raving about her Grandma Ruth's recipes.

They were family favorites and had never failed to garner praise.

All too soon it was time for Asher to head back to Chicago. His flight back to Brazil was booked for Christmas Eve.

Everly walked him to the car and stood next to the driver's-side door. Parting was as hard now as it had been on the dock in Manaus.

"I'll be back in three months," he promised, holding her, his hands knotted at the small of her back. "And not a day longer."

"It'll feel like an eternity."

He nodded, agreeing with her. "If they're able to hire another naturalist before, then I'll return sooner." He looked regretful.

"Are you sure about leaving the cruise line, Asher?" She hated the thought of him giving up what he loved most.

"It's no sacrifice when it means I'll be with you." He kissed her then, and they clung to each other.

Stepping back from the car so Asher could drive away took all her resolve. As she stood in the gently falling snow, watching his car disappear down the driveway, her hand automatically went to the gold chain he'd given her. All at once, the answer, the one that had plagued her for days, came to her.

She made her decision about Easy Home and knew it was the right one.

EPILOGUE

Three Years Later

Everly looked at the computer screen and a huge smile broke out. "Hot dog!" she said aloud, and clapped her hands. After leaving Easy Home, Everly, along with her two sisters, had created their own company using Grandma Ruth's candy recipes. It had been a lot of work, sweat equity, and an investment in time, resources, and family history.

They rented space in the bakery kitchen in town where Lily worked until they could afford to build one of their own. They started small, selling the candy to local businesses to avoid the mistake of expanding too soon.

Everly's voice must have caught the attention of her sister Lily, because she stepped into the office. "What's got you this excited?"

"Look at this." Everly pointed to the computer screen.

Lily let out a low whistle. "Is that a typo?"

"Don't think so," Everly said. The order was enough to launch them nationwide. After nearly three years of hard work, they were finally getting the recognition they needed.

"What's all the commotion in here?" Rose asked, entering the room.

"We got another order from a Candyland distributor," Lily said, "and it's huge. Look at all those zeros."

This was exactly what they'd been waiting for. This meant they were going to need to hire extra help to manage this fulfillment.

Jack had purchased her half of Easy Home. He wasn't happy to see her go and blamed himself for insisting she take a vacation. Those funds had financed the start-up for the candy company, which they named Flower Girls.

Using her business contacts, Everly mailed out free samples. It didn't take long for the orders to start pouring in. Their top seller was Grandma Ruth's Christmas Fudge.

Everly hurried home to tell Asher the great news. They lived a mile down the road from the farm where Everly had been born and raised. Asher taught at the local community college and loved his job. He'd been offered a much-higher-paying position with the University of Chicago but turned it down. He didn't even consider taking the hour-long train ride into the city, preferring to spend that commuting time with Everly instead.

Especially now that she was pregnant.

"From the smile you're wearing, I suspect you had a good day," her husband said, kissing her softly.

"I had an excellent day," she assured him.

"How about you, Button?" he asked, pressing his hand against the large round shape protruding from her front. "Little Hyacinth."

"We are not naming our daughter Hyacinth," Everly protested. Asher had gone through an entire list of flower names for their yet-to-be-born daughter.

"How about Clover?"

"No!"

"Zinnia?"

"Asher!" she cried in frustration.

"What's wrong with Amaryllis? A nice alliteration with Adams. Amaryllis Adams."

"That's even worse."

"Daisy, we're due in a month. We need a name."

"What's wrong with Ashley?" That was the name she liked best, naming their daughter after her husband. Asher was the one who insisted on following tradition with a flower name.

"Holly?" he tried again. "That's a perfect name for a December baby."

"Holly," she repeated testing the name on her tongue. "Holly Ashley Adams . . . That's a name I can live with," she said.

Looking extremely proud of himself, Asher led her into the family room and helped her into a chair. Their Christmas tree was up and two big knit stockings hung from the fireplace mantel, along with one tiny bootie.

"Now tell me about this big order."

"It's for Grandma Ruth's Christmas Fudge. Lily has already got two girls from the bakery working on fulfilling it. We'll ship out in two days, which for us is a quick turnaround."

Asher kissed her brow. "If anyone can do it, it's the three of you."

She relished his praise. Everly would have thought it'd be impossible for her to work with her sisters. Surprisingly, they balanced one another out. Everly did the marketing and accounting, Rose handled the supply chain and quality control, while Lily did the hands-on cooking. They worked together as if they'd been a team their entire lives, and in some ways they had.

"How was your day?" she asked Asher as he sat on the side of the chair, one arm stretched out across the back and cupping Everly's shoulder.

Asher pressed his cheek to the top of her head. "I love this, Daisy. Seeing my students' eyes light up with excitement as they learn about nature and our mission to preserve and care for our world. I couldn't be happier to have made this career switch. And to think, it might never have happened if I hadn't fallen in love with you."

Finding Asher was all due to Annette and her act of revenge. When Everly arrived in the Amazon, she was convinced this was the worst thing that could happen to her. This was supposed to be a vacation? Despite everything, it had turned into the best thing to ever happen to her. She'd met Asher, fallen in love, reunited with her family, and begun the greatest adventure of her life.

All she could think now was how grateful she was to Annette.

Jingle all
the Way

Debbie Macomber, the author of *Cottage by the Sea, Any Dream Will Do, If Not for You,* and the Rose Harbor Inn series, is a leading voice in women's fiction. Thirteen of her novels have reached No. 1 on the *New York Times* bestseller list, and five of her beloved Christmas novels have been made into hit movies. Macomber's Cedar Cove books have also been made into an original television series. There are more than 200 million copies of her books in print worldwide.

Join us at

For competitions galore,
exclusive interviews with our lovely
Sphere authors, chat about
all the latest books
and much, much more.

Follow us on Twitter at
🐦 @littlebookcafe

Subscribe to our newsletter and
Like us at 📘/thelittlebookcafe

Read. Love. Share.